The Real People
Book Five

THE LONG WAY HOME

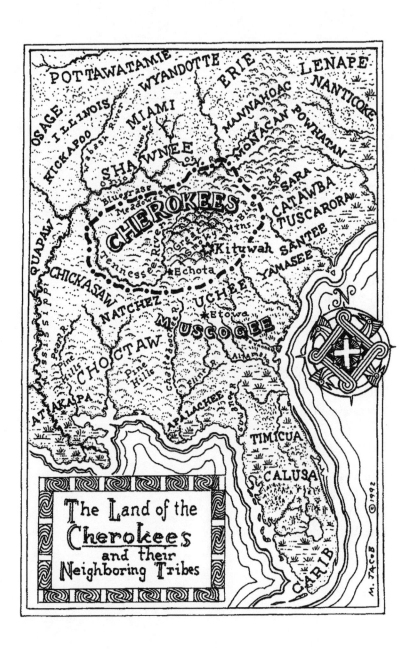

The Land of the Cherokees and their Neighboring Tribes

ROBERT J. CONLEY

The Long

Way Home

DOUBLEDAY

New York London Toronto Sydney Auckland

PUBLISHED BY DOUBLEDAY
a division of Bantam Doubleday Dell Publishing Group, Inc.
1540 Broadway, New York, New York 10036

DOUBLEDAY and the portrayal of an anchor with
a dolphin are trademarks of Doubleday,
a division of Bantam Doubleday Dell
Publishing Group, Inc.

Library of Congress Cataloging-in-Publication Data

Conley, Robert J.
The long way home/Robert J. Conley.—1st ed.
    p.   cm.—(The Real people; bk. 5)
1. Indians of North America—First contact with Europeans—
Fiction.   2. America—Discovery and exploration—Spanish—Fiction.
3. Cherokee Indians—Fiction.   I. Title.   II. Series: Conley,
Robert J.   Real people; bk. 5.
PS3553.O494L66   1994
813'.54—dc20   93-49679
CIP

ISBN 0-385-42621-6
Copyright © 1994 by Robert J. Conley
All Rights Reserved
Printed in the United States of America
September 1994
First Edition

10   9   8   7   6   5   4   3   2   1

THE LONG WAY HOME

One

THE OLD MAN moved slowly, as if each careful step was the last of a long and painful journey. In his right hand he carried, for use as a staff, a piece of a broken Spanish lance. And he leaned on the lance heavily.

He was a brown-skinned man, and age and weather and hardship had given his skin the look of old leather. His hair was gray and long, reaching about halfway down his back, and he was dressed in the manner of a Spanish *criado* or *sirviente*, a servant. He wore loose-fitting trousers that reached to just below his knees and an oversized tunic that hung below his waist halfway down to his knees and had short, loose sleeves. Both items of clothing were made of white woven cloth. On his feet were leather sandals.

He walked a road that he had traveled before, many times, but it had been years ago. How many years, he did not even know. And everything looked familiar to him but only as in a vaguely remembered dream. He knew, though, that his final destination was just over the next rise.

The muscles in his tired legs ached and the joints of his

hips creaked in pain as he made his slow way up the rise. He thought of stopping for a rest, of sitting down or even lying down, but he knew that if he did that, he would stay there, probably to die. And so he did not stop. He kept moving. He endured the pain.

At long last he reached the top of the rise, and he paused to look down into the valley below. There was nothing there. He stared wide-eyed and unblinking in disbelief, his mouth hanging open. He rubbed his rheumy old eyes with the back of his left arm. Still there was nothing there.

He asked himself if he could possibly be mistaken about the location, if he might be looking down into the wrong valley. After all, he reminded himself, it had been many long years. But no. There could be no mistake. He was on the right road, and he was looking down into the same old valley that he had once known so well. But Men's Town was no-where to be seen. It was gone. It was just gone.

He sat down heavily on the ground there on top of the rise and continued to stare at the spot where the town should have been, where he knew that it had been in times past, in the days of his youth. Of course, the Real People did move their towns from time to time, but not Men's Town. There could be no reason to move Men's Town. The *Ani-Kutani*, the priests of Men's Town, did not depend on the soil nearby for their food. Their food was all supplied by the people of other towns.

Yet Men's Town was gone, and he had no idea where to go to look for it. He did know where the next nearest towns would be—or should be. Perhaps they too had been moved. Strange things were happening in the world these days.

He thought back over the last three or four years of his life. He wasn't even sure how long it had been, how much time this journey had taken. He only knew that it seemed a lifetime, and that the hardships and the horrors he had experienced had aged him rapidly and prematurely. He recalled the number of recently abandoned towns he had seen while traveling with the Españols, the Spaniards, the Christians who burned everything they came across, who killed so casually and so brutally. Sometimes the people ahead of them had heard of their approach, and they simply abandoned their towns before the Spaniards arrived. Those had been the lucky ones.

Perhaps, he told himself, something like that was the explanation of the missing Men's Town. Hernando De Soto was not the only greedy Spaniard leading a band of would-be conquerors across the land. But here the whole town was just gone. Not abandoned. Not burned. Gone.

He raised himself back up to his feet, and as he did, he really felt the pain in his bones and muscles.

"Ah," he groaned out loud as he stood, partly out of an automatic reaction to the pains that shot through his body and partly out of conviction that the making of the noise somehow assisted him in his effort. He stood for a moment, breathing hard from the sudden exertion, and then started down into the valley.

It was a painful descent, but it was not as difficult as the going up on the other side had been. He was about halfway down the slope when he realized that he could, after all, see where the town had once been. He could see the outline of the old wall, and he could see the mound there where the temple had stood. He tried to envision the town as it had been, but he found that his memory failed him.

He tried to move faster, but could not. He kept his same slow, steady pace. Each step was an effort. Each step was deliberate and cautious. His mind told him that if he should chance to fall, his brittle old bones would surely break, and that would be the end. He was not afraid of the end, but he saw no reason to hasten it or to make it any more painful than was necessary. At last he reached the site of the vanished town.

"It was here," he said aloud, but in a low voice. After all, he was speaking only to himself. "It was right here."

And then he saw that the town had been gone for a very long time. The Spaniards could have had nothing to do with it. Whatever had happened to Men's Town, it had happened before their time.

"Ah, how long have I been gone?" he asked himself, but he did not answer. He did not know.

He walked to the place where his own house had been, and he stepped as if through the door. He stood there looking around, trying to see the walls and the roof overhead. It had been so long ago. He could not quite call up the image. Again he stepped carefully as if through the door, and walked over to the central mound.

He found where the steps that led to the top had been, but they had eroded almost away. He reached forward and put a hand on the mound, leaning there for a moment, trying to draw some strength from the mound, or some inspiration. Nothing came to him, and he turned and sat down on the ground, leaning back against the sloping surface of the ancient mound.

He let his old head fall back and rest against the earth, and he stared up into the sky. Ijodi was not far away, unless it too had been moved or destroyed. And Kituwah was not far. But he did not want to get up again. He did not want to walk anymore. It had been a long and difficult journey, and it was supposed to have ended here at Men's Town. He would stay. Soon, there at the base of the ancient temple mound, he drifted off into a deep and profound sleep.

. . . .

Three young men came over the rise. Two of them, one walking behind the other, carried a long pole, its ends resting on their shoulders. In the middle of the pole dangled a freshly killed deer carcass, its feet tied to the pole. The third man walked along beside them. All three were armed with bows and arrows. All three carried flint knives.

It was early in *gola*, the cold part of the year, so the young men all wore moccasins, leggings and matchcoats in addition to their breechclouts. Their heads were shaved except for their long, flowing scalplocks.

The young man who walked to the side had features which set him apart from the others. His skin was lighter and had a slightly different hue from that of his two companions, and his hair was not black, but brown with a tinge of red. His eyes were a steely blue-gray.

They were nearly to the bottom of the slope when the third man glanced over toward the site of the ancient priests' town, a town he had only heard tales about.

"Look," he said to his companions.

"What? Look at what?"

"Over there at the old mound," he said. "What is that?"

"It looks like some person lying down there."

"Let's go and see."

The three young men hurried over to the outline of the ancient town. The two put down their burden. All three looked at the impression left there in the ground by the old wall. They hesitated. It was not actually forbidden to enter the site, but the old stories of what had happened there gave the location a kind of ominous and sinister atmosphere in the minds of the Real People.

Then the one with the reddish-brown hair abruptly spoke. "Come on," he said. "Are you afraid?" And he stepped boldly across the boundary of Men's Town and headed for the mound. The other two looked at one another, hesitating.

" 'Squani's not afraid of anything," said one.

"That's because he believes in nothing," said the other.

"Shall we follow him?"

By that time the one they called 'Squani had reached the mound.

"Come on," he said. "There's nothing here to hurt you."

"What is it?" called one of his companions.

"Just a tired old man," said 'Squani. "Come on. He needs some help, I think."

Again the two looked at each other. Then one shrugged, and they went into the sinister zone. At the mound they found 'Squani squatting in front of an old man who was dressed strangely and who had long, nearly white hair. The old man sat on the ground and leaned back against the side of the mound. He did not seem to move at all.

"Is he alive?" asked one of the two.

"I think so," said 'Squani.

"What is he?"

"I don't know. I've never seen clothes like his. And look at this."

'Squani picked up the piece of lance that lay on the ground beside the old man.

"Is he a *'squani?*" asked one of the others.

"His skin is not white," said 'Squani, "and he has no hair on his face." He put a hand on the old man's shoulder and gently rocked. "Old man," he said. He shook the shoulder again, this time more energetically. "Old man. Can you hear me?"

Slowly the old head rolled just a bit against the mound. The eyes opened.

"Are you all right?" asked 'Squani.

The old man looked at 'Squani. Then he looked at the other two.

"Are you," he asked, "are you Real People?"

"Yes," said 'Squani. "We are. I'm called 'Squani. These are my friends, Buffalo Stand and Brush. Who are you?"

"A long time ago, I was known as Deadwood Lighter. I've not heard that name spoken for many years now. I've not spoken my own language for many years. Not until this moment."

"Then you too are a Real Person? One of us?" said Brush.

"I used to be," said the old man. "Perhaps I will be again before I die."

"You need food," said 'Squani. "We'll take you with us to Kituwah."

"Ah," said Deadwood Lighter. "Is Kituwah still there?"

"Yes," said Buffalo Stand. "Of course."

"I didn't know. Things have changed so much."

"Can you walk?" asked 'Squani. "If I help you?"

"No. I don't know. I've walked so far now. I don't know if I can go any further. Perhaps this is where I should stay."

"No," said 'Squani. "We'll carry you to Kituwah. You'll be all right."

Buffalo Stand and Brush, at 'Squani's insistence, found another pole about the same length as the one they already had. They fastened their matchcoats between the poles to make a litter, and they placed Deadwood Lighter on it. 'Squani slung the deer over his own shoulders, and his companions took up the litter. They started walking toward Kituwah.

Carrier was up on the climbing pole which leaned against the inside of the wall surrounding Kituwah. He saw them coming, and he knew that something was wrong. His son

'Squani was carrying a deer over his shoulders, and the other two young men seemed to be carrying a litter between them.

Carrier scurried down the pole and hurried toward the passageway that led beyond the walls. His uncle Dancing Rabbit saw him.

"What is it, nephew?" called Dancing Rabbit.

"My son is coming back," Carrier said over his shoulder. "His two friends are carrying something on a litter. Or someone."

Dancing Rabbit followed Carrier as quickly as he could, leaning on his cane and limping along. By the time he got outside the town, Carrier was already talking to the young men.

"What is it?" said Dancing Rabbit.

"We found this old man there at Men's Town," said Brush.

"Is he hurt?"

"Just tired and weak, I think," said Carrier. "Come on. We'll take him to your mother's house."

"All right," said 'Squani.

Dancing Rabbit turned as soon as he reached the others. They had not stopped walking. Now the whole group moved back toward the town. Dancing Rabbit took up the rear. 'Squani slowed his own pace to walk beside his father's uncle.

"His clothes are strange," said Dancing Rabbit. "Did you talk to him at all?"

"Yes. We talked for a little while. He's one of us. He's one of the Real People, but he's been gone for a long time. 'For many years,' he said."

"Did he tell you his name?"

"Yes. He said that he used to be known as Deadwood Lighter."

Dancing Rabbit stopped walking. He stared in astonished disbelief as the others moved on closer to the walls.

"Deadwood Lighter," he said. "Could it be? He seems so old. Could it really be that Deadwood Lighter has come home at last after all this long time?"

Two

THEY FED Deadwood Lighter, and they were astonished at how much food the withered old man could eat. Then they let him sleep. He slept for the rest of that day and all through the night. 'Squani was afraid for a time that the old man might have died in his sleep, but the following morning he was awake and up with the others, and he wanted to start his day by going to the water.

"It's been too long since I've been able to start the day in the proper manner," he said.

Almost all of the residents of Kituwah went to the river to start the day, and most of them stole glances at the strange old man who had come among them the day before. They had all heard about him by then. They had heard that he was one of their own who had been gone for many years. They had even heard his name: Deadwood Lighter.

As they waded into the cold running water, some of them talked about him.

"Do you know who he is?"

"No. They say that his name is Deadwood Lighter, but I've never heard of such a man."

"He speaks our language well enough, they say."

"Have you seen him?"

"No. I only heard the talk."

"I saw him yesterday when they carried him in. I thought that he was dead."

"Look to the left. He's going in the water just now."

"Where?"

"He's down there with Dancing Rabbit, Carrier, Potmaker and 'Squani. It was 'Squani who brought him in."

" 'Squani and the others, Brush and Buffalo Stand. They had gone hunting."

"Ha. I'll bet they didn't think they would find something like that."

"Do you see him now?"

"Yes. He has long hair. I see him."

"When I saw him yesterday, I thought that he was dead."

"Who is he, do you think, this Deadwood Lighter?"

"I don't know. Someone said that he was once a *Kutani*."

Back at the house of Potmaker and her family, Dancing Rabbit and his sister Walnut, Carrier's mother, came to visit. Dancing Rabbit presented Deadwood Lighter with a short clay pipe and a pouch of tobacco, and the old man lit the pipe with a coal from the fire. Dancing Rabbit studied the old face for as long as he dared.

"Yes," he said at last, "I believe that you really are my old companion Deadwood Lighter come back to us after all these years. Only—"

"Only you didn't think I would be so old?" said the other. "I'm old before my time. My experiences have made me so."

Dancing Rabbit looked at the ground. The old man exhaled a cloud of smoke and glanced at Dancing Rabbit.

"The years haven't changed you so much, my old friend," he said. "I would know Like-a-Pumpkin anywhere."

"But his name is changed," said Carrier. "My uncle is now known as Dancing Rabbit."

The old man puffed on the pipe and watched the smoke as it rose.

"It's been a long time since I've tasted good tobacco like this," he said. Then he glanced toward Dancing Rabbit. "Under any name," he said, "I never thought to see you again. I thought that you were dead."

"And I feared much the same for you," said Dancing Rabbit. "It's good to see you alive and here at home."

Deadwood Lighter sighed a heavy sigh.

"Thank you, my old friend," he said. "It's good to be here, if only for a short while longer. A man should die at home, unless he dies in battle."

"Uncle," asked Carrier, "is this one of the men you went west with that time you were looking for the house of Thunder? All those years ago?"

"Yes, nephew," said Dancing Rabbit. "Back in the days of the *Ani-Kutani*, when the priests ruled the Real People, we had a terrible drought. We tried all the ordinary ways to make the rains come, yet they did not come. So Standing-in-the-Doorway, who was the head of all the *Ani-Kutani*, picked three of us to go west to search for the house of Thunder and bring back the rain."

Dancing Rabbit glanced toward Deadwood Lighter and saw that the old man was slowly nodding his head. His eyes had a faraway look, and Dancing Rabbit knew that his one-time companion was recalling those old days as they talked. He continued his story.

"I was one. Deadwood Lighter here was the second. The third man was called—" He hesitated a moment before speaking the name. "Water Moccasin."

"Yes," said Deadwood Lighter, but he did not seem to be speaking to anyone in the room. "We were the three."

"We traveled west," said Dancing Rabbit. "We had no idea other than that about where to find the house of Thunder. Just west. And we had little trouble until we were caught by the Fierce People."

"The Fierce People?" said 'Squani. "Who are they?"

"I don't know," said Dancing Rabbit. "They speak a strange language and have strange ways. I call them the Fierce People because of their behavior, and because I know nothing else to call them."

"I learned their language eventually," said Deadwood Lighter. "They call themselves 'the People.' That's all. But Fierce People is a good name for them."

"They live far to the west," Dancing Rabbit continued. "I don't know how many days we had traveled before we met them."

"Nor do I," Deadwood Lighter added. He puffed on the pipe, but the tobacco had been used up. He tapped it out into the palm of his hand and reached for the pouch to fill it up again. "It was so long ago. Time is of no significance anyway."

"So, then, the Fierce People captured us," continued Dancing Rabbit, "and they made us their slaves. They took us to a village of tiny hovels where they lived in appalling filth. They made us do all the work, and they beat us.

"They took Deadwood Lighter away somewhere, and I never saw him again until yesterday. I did see Water Moccasin, though. His master was particularly brutal. Actually, he had two nasty women, and they were worse than he. One afternoon, poor Water Moccasin could stand it no longer, I guess. He ran, and they shot him in the back with an arrow. They left him there for the dogs to eat."

"I never knew what happened to him," said Deadwood Lighter. "But I thought that he was probably dead. Of course, I thought that you, Like-a-Pumpkin—excuse me, Dancing Rabbit—I thought that you were dead too."

The two former priests, former traveling companions and fellow sufferers, sat in silence, lost in their own secret thoughts of those days long ago. Carrier felt that the story should go on, so at last he spoke up into the uneasy stillness.

"But you escaped, Uncle," he said, "by imitating the rabbit in the story that tells how Jisdu escaped from the wolves."

"Yes," said Dancing Rabbit, with a small grin. "I did the rabbit dance and sang his song, and I killed the brute that had killed our poor companion."

"Oh," said Deadwood Lighter, his face brightening up a bit, "so that's how you got your new name?"

Dancing Rabbit chuckled. "Yes," he said.

"So then you escaped and found your way back home. I'm glad to learn that. But what has become of Men's Town?"

"While we were gone," said Dancing Rabbit, "the people rose up against the *Ani-Kutani*. Standing-in-the-Doorway had taken the young wife of a man from Ijodi, a man named Edohi. He killed her there on the wall at Men's Town in front of all the people during a big ceremony to make it rain. Of course, I didn't see that. I heard about it later.

"Edohi had been out hunting when it happened, and when he found out about it, he led the revolt. I arrived home just as it was ending. I found Men's Town in flames, and all of the priests were dead. All but me. And some of the people would have killed me right then and there, but Edohi said that there had been enough blood spilled. Until I saw you yesterday, I thought that I was the last *Kutani*."

Again the small group fell silent. The story of the fall of the priests was well known to all of the Real People, yet it was a tale of such import, of such magnitude, that its retelling almost always resulted in a hushed and profound silence, like a quiet, unspoken dread.

Deadwood Lighter had learned much from the tale, but the others had learned little, only that Deadwood Lighter had managed to acquire the tongue of the Fierce People and then somehow had survived his ordeal and returned home at long last. The rest of the story, told by Dancing Rabbit, they had heard before.

Deadwood Lighter sucked deeply at the pipe stem which was stuck between his lips, until clouds of blue-gray smoke obscured his weathered old face from the vision of the others in the room.

"Now I too have a tale to tell," he said, "but it's a tale for all of the people to hear at once. Spread the word for me, and send out to the other towns for all who want to listen. Tell them to come here to Kituwah and gather in the townhouse. It's a long tale, painful and frightening, and I'm a tired and weak old man. I'll tell it but once."

Dancing Rabbit glanced toward his nephew Carrier and stood up. Carrier also stood.

"Come on, nephew," said Dancing Rabbit. "Let's do as Deadwood Lighter asks and spread the word."

Everyone left the house except the old man and 'Squani. 'Squani moved a little closer, but of course, he looked at the ground, not up at the old man's face. To stare another in the face was rude at least; at most it could be threatening.

"Uncle," he said respectfully, "I'll go too and help to spread the word, but first I want to ask you something."

Deadwood Lighter looked for a brief moment through squinty eyes into the young man's face.

"Yes?" he said. "What do you want to ask?"

"When you tell your story," said 'Squani, "will you talk about the *Ani-'squani?*"

Deadwood Lighter looked puzzled.

"I don't know any such people," he said. "What did you call them?"

"*Ani-Asquani,*" said the young man, speaking more precisely. "You know. The white men."

"Oh. Is that what we're calling them? *Ani-Asquani,* is it? I had not heard them called that. They call themselves Español. You see, in my long absence, I learned their language too."

'Squani tried to say the word he had heard Deadwood Lighter use, but he couldn't make the sounds. It came out much as he had said it before.

"*Asquani,*" he said.

Deadwood Lighter nodded in recognition of the linguistic transfer he had just heard.

"Yes. Of course," he said. "*Ani-'squani.* You're saying 'Español.' But your name. Your name sounds like—"

"Yes," said 'Squani. "It is. My father, Carrier, went south to trade. It was there he met my mother, Potmaker. She is a Timucua woman. While he was down there, the *Ani-'squani* came. They captured Potmaker. She was rescued later, and Carrier brought her home with him and married her. He has been my father all my life, but he's not my real father."

"I see," said Deadwood Lighter.

"They gave me a real name when I was born, but the people have always called me 'Squani, because of who my father was."

"And you are curious to know more about these men whose blood runs in your veins?"

'Squani stared at the ground between his feet.

"Yes," he said.

"When you listen to my story," said Deadwood Lighter, "you'll hear more about the Españols than you'll want to know. Heed the advice of an old man, one who has lived long and traveled far. Your father is Carrier. Your mother is Potmaker. You are one of the Real People. Don't seek beyond that."

"*Wado*, Uncle," said 'Squani, and he left the house, but as he walked along the street, he tried to make the sounds he had heard the old man use. He tried to say the foreign word, "Español."

Dancing Rabbit had not gone far. He had stopped at the nearest neighbors to give them the message from Deadwood Lighter, and as he talked to them, he kept looking over his shoulder toward the house of Potmaker. He finished his chore there and paced impatiently for a moment, watching the house. Then he went to the next nearest neighbor.

He had given them the information and was limping along the road when he saw 'Squani leave Potmaker's house. He hobbled back as quickly as he could go. Deadwood Lighter looked up as Dancing Rabbit came back into the house.

"I wanted to see you alone," said Dancing Rabbit.

"What is it?"

"You remember what I was?"

"We were all *Ani-Kutani*."

"Yes, but I. Do you remember? Why was I selected to accompany you and Water Moccasin to the west?"

"Because you were a scribe," said the old man. "You could write the story of our journey."

"Yes. That. No one else knows. When I came back, the blood of the others, all the other *Ani-Kutani*, was still flowing. It was still warm. I barely escaped the wrath of the people. For a long time I lived in fear that someone would change his mind and decide to kill me after all. I was the last one, or so I thought."

"I can understand that," said Deadwood Lighter.

"So I kept quiet about the writing. No one knows."

Dancing Rabbit felt a little guilty at lying to his old companion. It was not quite true that no one knew. He had taught the writing to his nephew Carrier after having sworn the lad to secrecy. And now that Carrier was grown, Carrier had taught the system to his adopted son 'Squani. They would keep the writing from being completely lost, but they would keep it a secret. Dancing Rabbit was still afraid that if the secret got out, the old anger at the priests would surface once again. Someday, he thought, perhaps many generations hence, the *Ani-Kutani* would no longer be a memory. It would be nothing but an ancient tale. Then it might be safe for the secret to be let out, but for now it must be kept.

"And you want me, too, to keep quiet about the writing?" said Deadwood Lighter. "Is that it?"

"Yes. Tell them everything else, but do not tell them about the writing."

"Don't worry, old friend," said Deadwood Lighter. "The writing means nothing to me, and it has nothing to do with my story. Your secret is safe. It can die with you, for surely I will go before you do."

"Good," said Dancing Rabbit. "*Wado*. And now I'll get back to the business of informing the people of your intentions."

He turned and limped back out the door, and Deadwood Lighter reached again for the pouch of sacred tobacco.

Three

THE WORD had spread far and rapidly about the strange old man who had come home after so many years, and the townhouse was full of people, not just the people of Kituwah, but people from other towns as well; from Ijodi, Nikutsegi, Tellico, Hiwassee, from towns all over the country of the Real People. They had been coming in for days. Those who had arrived early had stayed as guests, either of clansmen, staying in their homes, or of the town, staying in the townhouse, waiting for the big event. Most had come in, however, on the very day that Deadwood Lighter planned to present his tale.

In the home of Walnut, the old man waited until late in the evening before he finally said that he was ready, and then Carrier sent out the word, and the people swarmed into the townhouse. Some were not able to get inside. They crowded around the door, part of a larger crowd that was forced to remain outside. They would have to get the story later, secondhand, from someone who had been lucky enough to get in.

Then Deadwood Lighter, accompanied by the still hobbling Dancing Rabbit, emerged from the house of his hosts and started walking toward the townhouse. They walked side by side, each leaning on a walking stick, one because of a crippled leg, the other because of the frailty of age and wear. Someone in the back of the outside crowd was the first to see their approach.

"Here he comes. He's coming now."

"The old man's coming."

"Dancing Rabbit is bringing him along now."

"Make room so that they can get through here," someone said.

"Look at them," said another. "Two men coming toward us on six legs."

A few chuckled at the joke. Then, as the two former priests approached nearer, the crowd split apart, making an aisle for them to walk through to the door of the townhouse. As they entered the aisle, the crowd, outside and inside, grew respectfully silent. The two men moved slowly and deliberately through the crowd, into the townhouse, up to the place of honor. Dancing Rabbit stood first before the people gathered there.

"Some of you may remember this man," he said. "Most of you will not, I think. I think, though, that most of you do know the story of how I went west years ago in the days of the *Ani-Kutani*, how I went west with two others to search for the house of Thunder but was captured by the Fierce People and later escaped. You know that one of my companions was killed and that I never saw the other again.

"I never saw him again until just recently when he came back to us, that day he was brought back to us by 'Squani and Buffalo Stand and Brush. This is the man, here beside me. His name is Deadwood Lighter, and he has called us all together here to listen to his tale about those years when he was away from us. He has seen much, and what he has seen is going to be important to us all. It should concern us all, so hear him well, my friends."

Dancing Rabbit walked away and found himself a seat, squeezing in between Carrier and 'Squani, and Deadwood Lighter stood alone before the crowd. He looked very old and very small. Dancing Rabbit wondered if the old man would find enough energy in his dry, old body to make his voice heard by the large crowd. And he wondered again just what his friend must have suffered to make him seem so old. Deadwood Lighter looked slowly around the room. He seemed to be searching for familiar faces. Then he opened his mouth wide and took a deep breath. At last he spoke.

"In the old days, I was a *Kutani*," he said. "We needed rain, and so we were sent by Standing-in-the-Doorway, who was our leader in those days, to find the house of Thunder, to bring back the rain. I and Water Moccasin and Like-a-Pumpkin, he you know today as Dancing Rabbit.

"We did not know where Thunder lived, except that he lived in the west, and so we walked west, farther west than any of us had ever been before. We were all afraid. None of us knew what waited for us in the west. But we went on. Eventually we were taken captive by the people we called the Fierce People. They took us to their village, beat us and made us their slaves. There I was separated from my two companions. I had no idea what had become of them. I thought them both dead.

"Those people, the Fierce People, kept me for a long time, so long that I was able to learn their language. I had a master who was called Stinking Dog. He didn't have me for long, though. He soon lost me in a game of chance to another, one they called Grease.

"One day we packed up everything and moved. We traveled across the prairie until we came to the village of another people, and there they traded. Grease sold me to a man of the other people. Once again I was a slave to people whose language I could not understand. But once again, I learned the language.

"I should tell you now that one of the reasons Standing-in-the-Doorway had selected me in the first place to make the journey in search of the house of Thunder was because of my talent for learning languages. In my youth, I could speak the tongues of all our nearby neighbors, the *Ani-Chahta, Ani-Cusa, Ani-Tsiksa,* and I could speak the trade language as well. I even knew our own ancient language, which, of course, had become the language of our rituals and ceremonies. That was my specialty as a *Kutani.*

"When I learned the language of my new captors, I found that my new master's name was Strong Bow. He was a brave warrior and a fairly decent man, but I was still a slave, and I was not treated much better than a dog. But then Strong Bow did not kick his dogs too often.

"I think that he almost liked me. He seemed to marvel at my ability to speak his language in a relatively short period of time. He fed me well, and now and then he even sat down to talk with me. He asked me where I came from, and I said I came from the east. He asked me what my people were called, and I said the People. Of course, that was what his people called themselves. For some reason I did not think it wise to allow anyone to know too much about me.

"Strong Bow's people lived mainly on *yansa,* but the buffalo out west are smaller than the ones we know here, and they're easier to kill. They're not so shy as the ones we know, so it's easier for the hunter to get close to them. And they travel in great herds, much larger than we ever see in these parts.

"Those people use the buffalo for their food. They use his bones and horns to make their tools and weapons. They live in cone-shaped lodges which they cover with his skin. And they grow no food. They trade with others who do grow food, or sometimes they steal from them.

"I stayed with these people for a long time, so long that I began to believe that I would die among them. And I had begun to feel old. The life of a slave does that to one, it seems. I even, from time to time, found myself wishing for death, longing to travel to the other side of the Sky Vault to find the Darkening Land, and I wondered if I would find my two lost companions there.

"But then there came a time when we packed up the camp to move again. This time we traveled a long way, going mostly south and a little west. At last we stopped at a town where the people lived in houses made of mud baked hard in the rays of the Sun. Some houses were stacked on top of other houses, and the people who lived on top had to climb up into their homes with long ladders.

"These people grew corn in many colors, and they traded with the buffalo hunters. I was just getting used to their strangeness when I saw something even more strange. There came among these Southwest people a people like none I had ever seen before. They were all male, and they had thin, pale skin, sickly pale, that burned and blistered in the Sun.

"My friends, you know who it is I speak of, for some of you have seen them by now, and I understand that you had heard about them before you ever saw them. But imagine, if you can, the position I was in. I had not even heard about them, and there they were before my eyes, looking terrible and making loud noises.

"Some of them had red hair, some yellow, some brown and some black. Their eyes, too, were a variety of colors: brown, blue, green, gray. Some of them had straight hair and some had hair that was wavy, some curly, even kinky like the hair on the head of *yansa*. Many of them even had hair on their faces. And they stank. I think they did not like water.

"Their clothing was like none I had ever seen before, and some of it was even made of metal, a very hard and shiny metal. Their language sounded harsh and ugly to my ears. But the strangest thing of all, and by far the most frightening, was the fact that some of them rode on the backs of great stamping, snorting beasts. The beasts, too, had clothing, and they did the bidding of the men.

"I was afraid of these men. Imagine, then, my horror when Strong Bow, my master, informed me on our second day in that village of stacked houses that he had sold me to one of these white, hairy men. I wondered what they would do with me. I wondered why they wanted me. It occurred to me that they might kill me and eat me. They had the great beasts to carry their burdens. Why did they need a slave?

"Then I supposed that they might need slaves after all for such chores as gathering wood and cleaning up, much the same as my previous captors. So I tried to be brave. But still, when the white man came to get me, I almost fainted away from fright.

"He was at least a hand taller than I and powerfully built. His skin was very light and blotchy, and his hair was red, both on top of his head and on his face. His eyes were a watery blue, and his teeth were bad. He rode on one of the great beasts, a black one, and carried at his side a long knife. He was younger than I, but the white men are no respecters of age.

"At first he kicked me and pushed me to make me understand where he wanted me to go, but once we had settled in one of the little mud houses, he was not so brutal. It took me a few days to realize what he was doing, what he wanted of me, for he was not giving me chores to do.

"Instead, he would pick something up and hold it out in front of him and say a word. He would say the word over and over. Eventually I would try to repeat the word. That was sometimes difficult, for there are sounds in his language that do not exist in ours, but I kept trying, and at last I could make them all.

"He was teaching me his language, and eventually I learned that was the very reason he had purchased me from Strong Bow. My former master had told him of my ability to learn languages. And I did learn. I learned even this strange and difficult language in a fairly short time. My new master was pleased.

"They called themselves and their language *Español*, a word that, I have learned since coming home, you have been calling *Asquani* in our language. My new master's name was Viviano García, and he owned the title of *Capitán*, which meant that he had won war honors among his own people.

"And he gave me a new name, one in his own language. I became Juan José, which means to them 'God Is Gracious' and 'Increaser,' but I don't think that Capitán García meant anything by that.

"The Españols—the *Ani-Asquani*—are very careless with their names, and I think that he called me Juan José only because both of those names are very common among them, and that was a way he had of showing me that I was of little importance.

"As I learned the language, I grew used to Capitán García. I learned his ways, and I was no longer afraid. My new life was easy and comfortable, especially when compared to what

I had been suffering. I was no longer sent out to do chores. I was not beaten and kicked. My hands and feet were no longer bound. I was fed well and regularly, and I slept inside on a soft mat, in the same room in which the *capitán* slept.

"I actually began to feel almost content with my new situation. I did notice that the *'squanis* were sometimes brusque, even rude, to their hosts, the people of the stacked mud houses. Now and then one might even show signs of brutality, if angered. They did not behave as if they were guests. They acted more like they were the masters of everything and everyone in sight.

"I confess, though, that I did not worry too much about their arrogant behavior, nor about the rude treatment our hosts received at their hands. My own situation seemed much improved, and I was thankful for that. I was thinking only about myself. I still had much to learn."

Four

DEADWOOD LIGHTER was tired. He sat down to rest. Some members of the crowd got up to stretch their legs, some walking around inside the townhouse, others going outside. Some of the people who had not been able to get inside took advantage of the milling around to steal into the house and find a seat for themselves.

Outside, children ran around the townhouse, played in the *gatayusti* field, and generally acted like children. Some people went to their homes to get something to eat. Men lounged around the townhouse, both inside and out, smoking their pipes. 'Squani spoke low, as if in confidence, to his adopted father, Carrier.

"Father," he said, "the old man can speak the language of the *Ani-Asquani*."

"Yes," said Carrier, "so he said."

"I wonder if he would teach me."

"Why would you want to know the language of the *Ani-'squani?*" asked Carrier.

"Oh," said 'Squani, "I don't know. If there are so many of

them, and they keep coming into our country, perhaps it would be of use one day."

But he thought: A *'squani* was my father. I am called 'Squani by everyone who knows me. I am half *'squani*. And I want to know. I want to know.

"Well," said Carrier, "Deadwood Lighter is old and tired. He might not want to have the trouble of teaching."

"Yes," said 'Squani. "Probably he wouldn't."

The crowd began to settle down again when they noticed the old man stand up. Soon the quiet had spread throughout, and the silence waited for Deadwood Lighter. He cleared his throat. He looked around the crowd. He took a deep breath.

"I learned the language," he said, "well enough to get along. And then one morning, the *capitán* woke me up early with a swift kick.

" 'Get up, Juan José,' he said. 'We're moving out today.'

" 'Moving out?' I said, sitting up and rubbing my eyes. 'Where are we going?'

" 'We're going to the ships,' he said, 'and then we're going to Habana.'

"Of course, I had no idea what a ship might be, and I had never heard of this place called Habana. But I crawled quickly out of my pallet and started to help the *capitán* to pack his belongings. I, myself, had next to nothing to pack. A change of clothing was all.

"My master's things were all put into a large box with a lid, and the box was loaded into a cart, a thing like a big box which rolls along on wheels. The cart was pulled by a beast they called an ox. It was something like a buffalo, but it was tame, and it had short hair.

"Then the *capitán* made me ride in the cart with his trunk. Another man drove the cart. I still have no idea who the man was, but I think that he must have been another slave. The *capitán* himself climbed up onto the back of his huge *caballo*. That is what they call the beast you have been calling *sogwili* in our language, *sogwili*, because it carries things on its back.

"He rode away swiftly to somewhere near the head of the column. We in the cart were kept to the rear to breathe the heavy dust stirred up by all the rest. I thought about jumping out of the cart to run away, but there were too many Españols around watching. On the backs of their *caballos*, they would have run me down in no time.

"So I rode on in the cart, swallowing dust with every breath. In the evening, before the Sun had crawled under the Sky Vault to the other side, we stopped to camp, and the *capitán* rode back to find me. He made me set up his tent and roll out our pallets. Early the next morning we were up, packed again and started again on our way.

"We traveled in this manner for several days, until we came to the big water. They called it *el océano*. I couldn't see well for a while because I was still in the cart at the end of the line, and there was a cloud of dust between me and the big water.

"But when I did see it, I was amazed. I had seen the big water to the east once in my youth. Still, the big water is always an overwhelming sight. But there was more. Out on the water were two big boats, bigger than any I had ever seen or even thought about. They called them *barcos*, and they were just sitting there, riding the waves.

"We camped the night there on the shore with the *barcos* out on the water in front of us, and the next morning, we loaded everything we had onto the boats. The *Ani-Asquani* even managed to get their beasts, the *caballos* and the oxen, their vicious dogs, all onto the *barcos*. And then all of us.

"We sailed southeast. We had not been long on the water,

when I became ill. I leaned over the edge of the *barco* so that I would vomit into the water instead of onto the floor, and while I was hanging my head like that, Capitán García came to stand beside me.

" 'What's the matter, Juan José?' he asked. 'Are you sea-sick?'

"I groaned and gagged, and the *capitán* laughed at me. He threw back his head and laughed and laughed. When at last he stopped laughing, he slapped me on the back. I coughed a few times.

" 'You'll get over it,' he said. 'It happens to most people their first time aboard ship.'

"Then he turned and walked away, laughing again. I suppose I was a funny sight to see that way, but I didn't feel funny. Not just then. I was sick for the rest of that day and into the night, but the following morning, I was better. I even managed to eat a little. The day after that, I was just fine.

" 'Juan José,' said my master, 'we'll make a *marinero* of you yet.' That was his word for one who goes on the water, his word for *ama-edohi*. Yes, he told me, 'We'll make a *marinero* of you yet.'

"For several days we rode the *barcos* across the big waters, and for much of the time I was afraid, though I kept my fear to myself. I did not know that there was anything out there. I didn't know whether or not to believe in this Habana they talked about. I wondered if there would ever be an end to the water.

"But there was an end to it, and there is such a place as Habana. It's on an island far to the south of us. This island used to be inhabited by people with brown skin, people like us, but the Españols came there and took it over. They killed the people or made slaves of them, and the ones they made slaves, they eventually worked to death.

"The Españols have made their main town there at Habana. From there they go up to the land of the Calusas and the Timucuas and other people we know, and they try to capture them to use them as slaves. And they have some black men they have brought to Habana from some other place across the waters. These *Ani-guhnage* are also slaves.

"In Habana, Capitán Viviano García had a small room where we took his trunk and unpacked. There we settled into an almost pleasant routine. Each day I shined and oiled his *armadura*. That's the pieces of clothing made of metal. During the day he went out and walked around the town. Sometimes he took me with him.

"He sometimes went to a marketplace, sometimes to places where he could buy food which was already prepared to eat. And there were places where he could buy a strong drink called *ron*. Now and then he gave me a little of it. It burned my throat when I swallowed it, and it made my head feel light.

"Sometimes Capitán García would drink too much *ron*, and he would stagger, and his speech would be blurred. Eventually he would fall over into a deep sleep, and when he came out of it later, his head would hurt.

"In the evenings when the *capitán* was not drinking *ron*, we would sit and talk to improve my Español, and he even began to teach me how to write his language down. The Españols have little marks they call letters. Each letter stands for a sound in their language, so if a man knows the letters, he can write down anything he can say."

Here Deadwood Lighter stopped talking to catch his breath, and he glanced over at Dancing Rabbit where he sat beside Carrier. He saw the furtive look that his old companion gave to his nephew, and he knew that Dancing Rabbit was thinking of his secret, and he guessed that the former *Kutani* scribe had taught the secret to his nephew. His old lips turned up in a barely perceptible smile, and he took a deep breath in order to resume his tale.

"One night," he said, "I was alone in the room. I was practicing my writing. All of a sudden, Capitán Viviano García burst into the room. He held a bottle of *ron* in each hand.

" 'Juan José,' he said, 'tonight you and I are going to get drunk.'

" '*Capitán*,' I said, 'I don't think that I can drink *ron* the way you do. I'm afraid to drink enough of it to get drunk.'

"What he meant was that we would each drink so much of the *ron* that we would lose our senses and eventually pass out. I had seen the *capitán* like that often enough that I didn't want to experience it for myself.

" 'You'll do as I say, you swarthy *salvaje*,' said the *capitán*. 'Here. Take this.'

"He handed me one of the bottles, and he pulled the stopper out of the other and took a long drink from it. 'Go on,' he said.

"I pulled the stopper out of my bottle and put the bottle to my lips. I took a small taste. It burned my lips, my tongue, and it burned all the way to my stomach.

" 'Drink,' roared García. I turned the bottle up and took a swallow and almost choked with coughing. García roared with laughter. As soon as he was able, he took another drink, and he gestured at me to do the same. I did. It was not quite so bad as before. We continued drinking like that into the night, and the *capitán* began to talk more and more.

" 'Where are you from, Juan José?' he asked.

" 'North of here,' I said.

" 'What are your people called?'

" 'My people simply call themselves the People.'

"My head felt cloudy, but I was still able to think a little, and I still felt as if I should not let my captors know just exactly who I was or where I had come from. I'm not sure why I felt that way, but I did.

" 'How do you say that then,' García asked me, 'in your native language? How do you say *the People?*'

"I deceived him by speaking the word for *people* from the trade language. That seemed to satisfy him. He took another drink, and then he stretched himself out on his cot. I was sitting up in a chair. I had no cot. Even in the room in Habana, I was still sleeping on a pallet on the floor.

" 'Your talent for languages may come in handy very soon now, my poor wretch,' he said.

"I did not answer him. My head was reeling, and I was afraid that I was going to fall out of the chair. Even so I took another drink.

" 'Why do you think that we are getting drunk tonight?' he asked. 'You and I together. Why?'

" 'I don't know,' I said, and I could tell even in my stupor that my voice was blurred.

" 'Juan José,' said the *capitán*, 'in the morning we will pack our things.'

" 'We are leaving Habana?' I said.

" 'Yes. In the morning we will pack our things and take them to the dock. There we will board a *barco* under the command of the governor himself.'

" 'The governor?' I said stupidly, and I barely caught myself from falling over. I stood up, and my legs were weak and wobbly.

" '*Sí. El Gobernante.* The governor. The ruler of this

whole island. The famous Don Hernando De Soto, *Adelantado* of Cuba and Governor of Florida.'

"I took two dangerously unsure steps over to my pallet and managed to lie down heavily on my back. I still had the bottle clutched in my hand, and like a fool, I took another drink from it. The little room seemed to be spinning around and around.

" 'Do you even know of whom I speak?' said the *capitán*.

" 'No,' I said. 'Pardon my ignorance, *mi capitán*. I do not know.'

" 'Don Hernando is a great soldier, a conquistador. He was with Pizarro in Peru where he helped to conquer the Incas. Do you know of them?'

" 'I'm afraid that I do not,' I said. I thought that I was going to be sick, and I wanted to go to sleep before that happened.

" 'Don Hernando is a rich man because of his previous expeditions,' said García, 'and he is leading another expedition in search of even further wealth. Everyone who goes with him will become rich. And I am going along.'

" 'And I?'

" 'Yes, but, of course, you will not become rich. It doesn't matter. You wouldn't know what to do with gold if you had it. Do your people have gold, Juan José?'

" 'I'm not sure that I know what gold is,' I said.

" 'Bah,' said García. 'I don't know how you can stand to be so ignorant. Of all your people, you're the lucky one. You're able to learn from me. You might become halfway civilized eventually.'

"I felt the contents of my stomach welling up, and I turned and got myself up to my unsteady feet and headed for the door as fast as I could go. Outside, over the noise of my own retching, I could hear the *capitán* inside laughing uproariously. At least he was enjoying my misery.

Five

I T WAS with great difficulty that I arose the following
morning and packed the belongings of Capitán Viviano
García and then lugged his great trunk to the place at the
water's edge where the huge ships were waiting to be loaded
and to take us I knew not where. Of course, I didn't really
care at that moment where they might take me or what they
might do with me.

"I thought that I would surely die, I was in such misery.
My body ached all over as if I had been beaten with a stick,
and my head was throbbing with a regular, rhythmic pounding pain. It was because of the *ron* García had made me
drink. I was in no condition to pay much attention to what
was going on around me. It was all I could do to respond to
orders given directly to me, but I could see that the ships
were being loaded with people, four-legged animals and supplies.

"There were many *Ani-'squani* soldiers, and many *caballos*.
Then there were some of the *yansa*-like beasts, and finally
there were a few hundred of a beast I had not seen before.

They resembled *sikwa*, but they were much larger than the little grinning opossum. Their noses were flatter than his, and their tails were short and curled. The Españols called them *puercos*, and Capitán García said that they were for food, and they were all owned by the great Don Hernando De Soto.

"The Españols, who also call themselves *Cristianos*, don't hunt for their meat the way we do. They take the animals along with them in great herds, and when they get hungry, they kill one. At least, that's what García told me about the great herd of *sikwa*-like animals, but I'll tell you more about that later on.

"The men who had the responsibility of herding and loading the *sikwas* had a terrible time, for the animals ran grunting and squealing in all directions. With that and the other noises all around, I thought that my head would burst. But it did not, and eventually the ships were loaded, all nine of them. And soon they were sailing out to sea.

"I had been sick the first time I went on the water in one of the big boats, but it had been nothing compared to my misery this second time. I was suffering already from the *ron*. García called it a hangover. That combined with the rolling and pitching of the boat were more than I thought I would be able to stand.

"As I was hanging over the side trying to get rid of the vileness inside me, my master laughed at me unmercifully.

" 'You're learning how to be a civilized drinker, Juan José,' he said.

"I was unable to say anything to him in response. I was sick that way for two days. Then at last I was all right again, and once more I was able to eat. Still I was not able to walk well because of the pitching of the boat. García laughed at me for that as well. Once as we were walking along the deck, which is what they called the floor of the boat, there was a mighty lurch, and I fell over. After he had finally stopped laughing at me, García said, 'In a few days you'll get your sea legs.'

"We were on the water for twelve days, and then at last we landed. At first I had no idea where we were, but at least my master and I were among those who got off the boats and were at long last on dry land again. The Españols who went ashore set up a temporary camp, and once that had been done, a few of them got onto their *caballos* and rode away. We didn't see them again for a few days.

"When they came back, they had four women with them. I heard them say they had seen six '*Indios.*' That is a name that they have given to all of us: the Real People, the Timucua People, the Calusa People, the Choctaw People, all of the brown-skinned people who live in these lands. *Indios.*

"Anyway, they had come across six men. They killed two of them, and the others escaped. They did not say why they had killed the two, and no one bothered to ask them. It was as if the matter was of no importance. Then they had found the women and captured them to bring them back to where we were camped. We listened to their tale, and then Viviano García called me to his side.

" 'Juan José,' he said, 'see if you can talk to these women.'

"I decided that I would try the trade language on them rather than a series of specific tongues. Besides, my guess was that they were Timucuas, and I have never learned that language.

" 'Hello,' I said. 'Do you speak the trade language?'

"They were very frightened and did not respond at once. They stood huddled together, looking at the ground. I asked them again. One of them glanced up shyly toward me.

" 'Yes,' she said. 'I can speak it.'

" 'Who are your people?' I asked her.

" 'We are Timucua people from the village of Ucita.'

"Capitán Viviano García nudged me roughly on the shoulder.

" 'What did she say?' he demanded.

" 'She said that they are Timucua people, and that they come from the village of Ucita,' I told him.

" 'Ucita,' he said. 'Is that the name of the village then?'

" 'Ucita is the name of your village?' I asked the woman.

" 'No,' she said. 'Ucita is the name of our town chief.'

" 'The chief of their village is called Ucita,' I told García. He nodded his head very wisely. 'Mmmm,' he mused thoughtfully. Then another man broke in rudely on the conversation.

" 'Where is this place?' he said. 'How far from here?'

"I looked at my master questioningly, and he nudged me hard again with his elbow in my ribs.

" 'Go on,' he said. 'Ask her.'

"I turned back to the Timucua woman.

" 'Where is your town?' I asked.

"She pointed east.

" 'How far?'

"She shrugged. 'Not far. A day's walk maybe. No more than that.'

"I translated her words into the language of the Españols, and the rude man turned to García. His face was red, as if burning with anger.

" 'Take five men,' he said, 'and take her along for a guide.' He jerked a thumb toward the woman to whom I had been speaking. 'Take your talking slave with you. Find this village and come back to report to me.'

" 'Right away, Don Hernando,' said García, and then I knew that the rude man for whom I felt such contempt was none other than the governor himself, Don Hernando De Soto. 'Come along, Juan José,' my master said, turning again to me, 'and bring that woman with us.'

"While I was helping my master to arm himself, he asked me, 'How is it that you are able to speak with that woman? Is it your language that you were speaking?'

" 'We were speaking a trade language,' I said. 'It's a simplified tongue based on one of the local ones. Many different peoples make use of it in this area.'

" 'Then,' said García, 'we must be near your own people.'

" 'Not so near,' I said. 'My people are far to the north of here. If these people had been my near neighbors, I would undoubtedly have learned to speak their language. The use of the trade language is widespread.'

"I still did not want my captors to know too much about me, but by this time I was beginning to realize why I felt that way. I thought that perhaps if the *Cristianos* brought me close to home I might find a way to escape from them. And if they knew that we were actually getting close to my home, they would almost surely watch me very closely. So I kept my secret.

" 'Come along,' said Capitán García. He was fully dressed and armed. He ducked his head and went out of our tent without looking back. I turned to the woman, who had pressed herself into a far corner.

" 'Come with me,' I said.

"I followed the *capitán*, and she followed me. When we stepped outside, we saw the others waiting there for us. There were five *Cristianos*, all heavily armed and mounted on the backs of the beasts they called *caballos*, the ones you call *sogwili*. They were frightful-looking.

"One *sogwili* was standing there with a saddle on his back

waiting for my master to climb up on him. The woman and I were made to walk along beside my master and his beast. They did not go slow.

"We had to trot along all the way, and now and then we had to really run to keep up with them. By the time we reached Ucita's village, I was all out of breath. The young woman, though, didn't seem much the worse for the journey.

"When the people saw us coming they ran, and Capitán García called out to me.

" 'Stop them, Juan José,' he said. 'Tell them we want to talk. We mean no harm. We want to meet their chief.'

"I yelled out after the running Timucuas words to the effect of what my master had said. Some of them slowed down to listen. A few hid behind trees and looked back at us.

" 'Perhaps, *Capitán*,' I said, 'if the woman and I went ahead alone, we could talk to them.'

"García thought for a moment before he answered me.

" 'All right,' he said. 'Go talk to them. But if you try to escape from me, I'll chase all of you down and kill you. I'll feed you to the governor's dogs.'

"I turned to the woman.

" 'Come on,' I said. 'We have to go ahead and talk to your people. My master wants to meet with your chief. If we fail, he'll kill all of us. Come on. Come with me.'

"We walked slowly toward the frightened Timucuas. They looked at us with suspicion, but they didn't run. The Españols sat waiting on their beasts where we left them. As we walked closer to the edge of the village, one bold young man stepped out from behind a tree.

" 'Hello,' I said. 'Do you speak the trade language?'

"He only looked at me with a puzzled expression on his

face. I took that to mean that he did not, so I turned to the woman.

" 'Do you know this man?' I asked her.

" 'Yes,' she said. 'He's my uncle's son.'

" 'Speak to him,' I said, 'and tell him that everything's all right. Tell him that my master and the others want to meet your chief and talk. They mean no harm.'

"The woman spoke to the man in their Timucua tongue, and I could only assume that she told him what I had asked her to tell. I expect that she said a little more, though, than what I told her to say. He answered her, and I waited for them to pause. Then I spoke to her again.

" 'What did he say?' I asked.

" 'He said that he would go to Ucita and tell him what you said. He wants us to wait here.'

" 'All right,' I said. She spoke to him again, briefly this time, and he turned and ran into the village, disappearing around the corner of a house. We could see him no more, so we stood there waiting.

" 'Juan José,' my master yelled.

" '*Sí, Capitán?*'

" 'What the hell is going on over there?'

" 'The man has gone to tell Ucita what you said. He told us to wait here until he comes back.'

" 'He'd better come back,' said García, 'and soon, too. I'm running short of patience.'

"Just then, a man appeared at the edge of the village. I had never seen him before, but I knew right away that he must be Ucita, for he was dressed as only a town chief would dress. He carried himself proudly. All the parts of his body I could see were covered with tattoos, but I couldn't see his back and shoulders for they were draped over with a beautiful matchcoat of brightly colored feathers, and he wore a great many colored feathers on his head. Five men walked with him. One of them was the young man with whom we had spoken moments before.

"He took a deep breath, drew himself up even taller and walked toward us.

"When they were close enough, I spoke again to the young man, but through the woman for an interpreter.

" 'Tell your chief I greet him,' I said. 'My master, the Español, Capitán Viviano García, wants to meet him.'

"I gestured toward the *capitán*. Ucita and his followers stopped. The young man spoke to Ucita, and Ucita answered him with a word. Then the young man spoke again to the woman. She nodded and turned to me.

" 'He said for us to take him to your master,' she said.

"I turned and led the way, and the rest followed. In another moment I was standing beside García's beast, looking up at my master.

" '*Capitán*,' I said, 'this is Ucita, the chief of this town.'

" 'Tell Ucita,' said García, 'that I represent Don Hernando De Soto, Governor of all of Florida and *Adelantado* of Cuba, who has claimed all of this land for the majesties of España. Tell him that the *Adelantado* and all of his men will be coming here. We will stay in this village until we are ready to move on. We will expect to be fed and housed while we remain. Tell him that.'

"I told the woman. She told the young man, and he told Ucita. Of course, Ucita had understood what the young woman said, but we had established a pattern, and we stuck to it. All of us, I think, were astonished at what García said. After a terribly uneasy pause, Ucita spoke his response. The woman translated for me, and I turned to my master. I'm sure that he could read fear in my face.

" 'Well,' he said. 'What did he say?'

" 'He said that he does not know your governor, and he does not know you,' I said, and I think that my voice was quavering. 'He said, "Who does this man think he is to come here and give me orders?" '

M. J.

Six

THEN EVERYTHING happened so fast it made my head swim. It was as if it all happened at once. García was off his beast almost immediately. I don't know how he and the others moved so quickly, encumbered as they were with heavy weapons and armor.

"But García was behind Ucita with his left arm around the neck of the chief. His right hand held a knife at Ucita's throat. The others had out their *espadas*, as they call them, their long knives or swords, and they hacked at the men who had accompanied Ucita out to meet with us. It was horrible. In no time at all, four men were lying dead and butchered, and their blood was soaking the ground around their mutilated bodies.

"The young man and young woman through whom we had been talking to Ucita did not move at first. They stood, fascinated with fear. Then they turned as if to run.

" 'Tell them to stand still, Juan José,' said García, 'or I will cut his throat.'

" 'Wait,' I said in the trade language. 'If you run, my master will kill your chief.'

"The woman put a hand on the man's shoulder and spoke to him. They stopped and turned to stare at the grisly scene. García seemed to tighten his grip around the throat of Ucita, and he pressed the point of his sharp knife a little harder against the chief's throat.

" 'Now,' said García, 'tell them to go on into the town and tell their people that we're coming in. If they attempt to rescue their chief or if they try anything against us, I will kill him instantly. Tell them that.'

" 'My master wants you to go on into the town and tell the rest of your people what has happened out here,' I said in the trade tongue. 'Tell them that if anyone makes a move toward the white men, they will kill Ucita immediately.' Having said what my master had ordered me to say, I added a few words of my own. 'He will do it, if you fail to obey,' I said. 'These men are the most brutal I have ever seen.'

" 'Go with them, Juan José,' said García, 'and come back here and tell me as soon as they've delivered my message.'

"I followed the two dumbfounded Timucuas into the town. The town was not walled, and the houses were all made of wood frames and covered with grass. In the center of the town was a large townhouse. It was built much like the smaller houses, but on a larger scale.

"As we walked into the town, it occurred to me that the angry and frightened Timucuas might simply kill me in response to what had happened, since in their minds I was surely associated with the hated Españols.

"The people were all there, it seemed. No one had run away. They were standing in their doorways, peering out cautiously, or looking timidly around the corners of houses. We walked on to the center of the village.

"Then the young woman stopped and stood there in the middle of town. She spoke out in a strong voice and addressed the whole town in her own language. Of course, I could not understand. Some of the people looked at each other and muttered a few words. No one moved.

" 'Have you told them what my master said?' I asked her in the trade language.

" 'Yes,' she said. 'They will do nothing that could bring harm to Ucita.'

" 'All right,' I said. 'I have to go back to him, then, and tell him.'

"I turned and trotted back out of the town to where García waited. When I got there I saw that Ucita's arms had been tied behind his back.

" 'What did they say?' García demanded of me.

" 'They will do nothing against you,' I said. 'They do not want you to harm their chief.'

" 'Good,' said García. 'Then let's go.'

"García prodded Ucita along ahead of himself. One Español walked in front of them and one on either side. I and the other two walked behind, leading all of the *sogwilis*. We went into the town and immediately entered the townhouse. The people made no move against the white men. They could have easily overwhelmed them at that time, but their love of Ucita held them back.

" 'This place should serve us well,' said García. 'Juan José, get that woman in here with us to translate.'

"I found the woman outside where I had left her earlier and called her into the townhouse. She came at once. By then García was talking to another of the Españols, a man called Vásquez.

" 'Ride back to the governor,' he said, 'and tell him what

we've found here. The rest of us will wait here until you return with his orders.'

"Vásquez left, and García, through me and the woman, ordered that food be sent for us. He also called for more young women. All of what he asked for was sent. We stayed in the townhouse that night.

"The next morning De Soto came with all of his mounted men. He immediately took Ucita away from my master to hold as his personal hostage. He congratulated García on his good work, but then told us to move out of the townhouse and find a place for ourselves. He took over the townhouse for himself and kept with him only those men who were closest to him. The rest of us had to move out. We moved into various houses, putting out the owners to move in with their friends or neighbors. García and I and the young woman, our interpreter, took a house away from a family of six. I felt bad for them, but there was nothing I could do.

"Late that afternoon the rest of the Españols arrived, even those driving along before them the great herd of *sikwas*. The squealing animals ran in all directions, frightening the village people and nearly running the legs off their keepers.

"The rest of that day we did nothing but settle in. The villagers were forced to find and prepare enough food for all of the governor's men. The burden on them was terrible. If they had decided at that point that Ucita's life was not worth all they were going through, it was too late for them to do anything about it. There were too many Españols among them by then. They had no choice but to obey the demands of De Soto.

"The following morning, the governor sent for my master. García told me and the woman to follow along, so the three of us went back again to the townhouse. De Soto was sitting there in the chief's honored place, his filthy feet resting on the bare back of a naked Timucua woman.

" 'García,' he said, 'I want you to question this Ucita. Ask him where there is gold. Tell him if we don't find gold, he and all of his people will die slow and miserable deaths.'

"García turned to me. 'Tell the woman what the governor said and tell her to say the same thing to Ucita.'

"I told the woman, and she turned to speak to Ucita, but the chief interrupted her after only a few words.

" 'I understand the jargon,' he said, and then he spoke directly to me. 'Tell your cruel and greedy masters that we have no yellow metal here.'

"I translated Ucita's words, leaving out the 'cruel and greedy,' and this time it was De Soto who interrupted. 'Speak to me, *esclavo*,' he said. 'We don't need to go through so many different mouths.'

" '*Sí*, Governor,' I said.

" 'What name did García call you?'

" 'Juan José, Governor.'

" 'Well, Juan José, so this Ucita claims to have no gold. Is that what you said?'

" '*Sí*, Governor,' I said.

" 'Do you believe him?'

"I did not know what to say to that. In truth, I did believe Ucita. I have never heard of the Timucuas or any of their neighbors having the yellow metal, but if I were to tell the governor that, I thought, then the Españols might reason that I was somewhere close to my own home. I had told García only that I was from a place far to the north, and I was content to leave it at that. I shrugged.

" 'I don't know, Governor,' I said. 'This is a strange country to me and these people strangers.'

" 'Yet you are able to converse with these people,' said the governor, his voice betraying his suspicion.

" 'Yes, Excellency,' I said. 'We make use of a trade language which is widespread. Many people of different tongues use that simple language in order to communicate with one another.'

" 'What do you think, García?' said De Soto.

" 'If Ucita had gold,' said the *capitán*, 'would he admit it to us?'

" 'He might if his feet were roasting,' said the governor. Then he turned again to me. 'Stoke up the fire there,' he ordered.

"I was horrified at De Soto's threat, but I could think of nothing to do but obey. There was a small fire in the center of the townhouse, and there were pieces of wood nearby. I started to put more wood on the fire. I felt like a coward and a traitor to my own kind. Just then an Español came rushing in through the door.

" 'Governor,' he cried, 'pardon me for this interruption, but I thought you'd want to know about this immediately.'

"I put two more sticks on the fire and turned to watch and listen to find out what was so important.

" 'Well, what is it then?' said the governor.

"The man at the doorway stepped to one side and made a sweeping gesture with his arm back toward the door.

" 'Look what I have found in this village,' he said, 'living here among these savages.'

"Another man stepped in through the doorway to stand behind him timidly. The messenger pushed him forward. He was dressed like the Timucuas, but he was like the Españols in his physical characteristics. He had light brown curly hair, and his eyes were light. Hair grew on his face and on his body. His skin was darkened from the Sun, but the other characteristics gave him away for what he really was.

"De Soto leaned forward and stared hard at the man, seemingly in disbelief. He shoved away with his foot the naked woman who had been lying there before him, and he stood up.

" 'Bring him here,' he said.

"The man who had come in with the announcement took the other and led him up close to the governor. The governor looked at him for a long and quiet moment, then sat back down.

" 'What is your name?' he demanded.

" 'Juan Ortiz, Excellency,' said the timid man.

" 'Juan Ortiz,' said De Soto, 'explain to me your presence here and your appearance.'

" 'Sir, I came to this land with Narváez in 1527. Please, can you tell me, what year is it now?'

" 'It's 1539,' said the governor. 'Do you mean to tell me that you've been here among these people for twelve years?'

" 'I was lost and left behind by Narváez,' said Ortiz. 'I've been here ever since.'

" 'In this village?'

" 'This one and others like it. Others nearby. Others of the same people.'

" 'You speak their language?'

" 'Yes, Excellency. I had to learn it to survive here among them.'

" 'You know this man Ucita here?'

" 'Yes.'

" 'Ask him where he keeps his gold.'

"I knew, of course, what the governor was doing. He was checking to see if I had in truth asked Ucita what he had told me to ask. I knew what I had said and that I had translated truly, yet this trick of the governor's frightened me. I listened while Ortiz questioned Ucita, but I could not understand them, for they spoke in the Timucua tongue, not the trade language. Finally, Ortiz turned away from Ucita and back toward De Soto.

" 'He said that he has no gold,' said Ortiz.

" 'Is he lying, do you think?' asked the governor.

" 'I don't think so,' said Ortiz, and I breathed a sigh of relief. 'I have never seen any gold among these people. They are rich in food, but the few metals they have are common: mica and copper, I think. And most of that they get in trade with people who live to the north. They sometimes have pearls, but they are the freshwater variety, not as valuable as the other kind. I have found them to be a poor people in almost every way.'

"I myself thought that the Timucua people seemed rich enough, but then I had not yet quite learned how the Españols count their wealth. To these white people, the yellow metal is the most important thing on earth. If they have much of it, they are rich. They use it to buy things from each other. Anything they want, they can buy with the yellow metal. Nothing else in life is so important to them as possession of this metal.

"De Soto scowled at this unwelcome information. 'Where, then,' he said, 'is there gold to be found?'

"Ortiz turned back to Ucita and started to speak. The two of them talked for a short while together in the Timucua tongue before Ortiz turned back to the governor.

" 'He says that he does not know,' he said. 'He cannot be sure, but he thinks that maybe you would find what you're looking for if you go to a place called Paracoxi.'

" 'Paracoxi?' said the governor. 'Where is this place and how far?'

"Ortiz again spoke to Ucita and again turned back to the governor.

" 'It's north of here,' he said, 'no more than a day's journey.'

" 'Then we'll go to this Paracoxi,' said De Soto, 'but if we find no gold there, we'll come back here, and Ucita and all his people will die.'

Seven

I DON'T KNOW how the people of Paracoxi called themselves or their town. I think they were not Timucua people, so the word we first heard from Ucita to call them by was likely not their own. Then I never heard the word again from Ucita, only from the Españols, and they pronounced everything wrong.

"I don't know who the Paracoxi people were or if any of them are left alive. They lived north of Ucita's town but still far south of where we are here. I think that they may have been Apalachees or a people related to the Apalachees or affiliated with them in some way, but I don't really know.

"At any rate, the governor had been told that he might find gold at that place, and he was very anxious for it. Even so, he did not go himself. He sent for a man, one of his officers, called Baltasar de Gallegos, and ordered him to take fifty men mounted on *sogwilis* and thirty men on foot and go to Paracoxi to find the gold.

"My master and I and the woman, whom my master had begun calling Falda, were ordered to go along with the Gallegos expedition. The governor kept Ortiz with him there at Ucita's town. Thus, while we were gone, he still had a translator for his own use.

"Gallegos led us out the next morning. The men mounted on beasts were in the front, and the foot soldiers followed, eating their dust. García, my master, was one of the riders. Falda and I walked along beside the foot soldiers.

"Some of the foot soldiers led, by means of stout lines, big vicious dogs. These are not like any of the *gihlis* we have. I had never before seen such big and ferocious dogs. I got a little too near one of the beasts one time, and it came at me, barking and snarling and slavering. It looked and acted as if it wanted to tear me apart. I was glad that one of the Españols held it by its leash. When I jumped back frightened, he and the others around him laughed at me.

" 'That will teach you,' he said, 'to keep your proper distance.'

"I skulked back to the side of Falda and walked along with my head held down in shame.

" 'Juan José,' she said, for that is the only name she had heard me called, 'what will happen when we get there, do you think?'

" 'I don't know, Falda,' I said. 'Much depends on whether or not they find what they're looking for, I guess.'

" 'You mean the yellow metal?'

" 'Yes,' I said. 'I think the yellow metal means more to them than life itself or even than honor.'

" 'I'm frightened, Juan José,' she said.

" 'Yes,' said I. 'I'm afraid too. I don't know what to do. I never expected to face anything like this in my life.'

"We reached the place called Paracoxi late that evening, and the people who lived there were ready for us. They had somehow learned of the approach of the *Cristianos*, and as we drew near the town, arrows flew. Don Baltasar roared an order, and the mounted men charged the town. Those on foot raced along behind, waving their swords in the air and screaming.

"Falda and I were left behind, so we did not see exactly what was happening up there, but I had a pretty good idea. The noise of the fight was horrible. We looked at one another, the dread showing, I expect, on both of our faces.

" 'We could run away now,' I said. 'No one is watching us. They're all busy fighting.'

" 'If we run away,' Falda said, 'they might kill Ucita and others out of revenge. I'm afraid to stay, but I'm afraid to run away too.'

"Once again I was impressed with the love Ucita's people held for him. I had no reason to love Ucita, for I hardly knew the man, and certainly my own loyalties lay elsewhere. But when this brave young woman refused to run away, in spite of her fears, I was too ashamed to run. I stayed with her.

"Soon the noise of battle died down, and Falda and I walked slowly toward the town. I could see immediately that my sense of what had been happening over there had been correct. There were the mutilated bodies of the defenders of Paracoxi lying around the edge of the town, and the triumphant Españols stood around or sat on the backs of their beasts holding their dripping, blood-drenched weapons.

"The survivors of Paracoxi stood unarmed, dejected and frightened, prisoners of the *Cristianos*. Out in front of the others, Baltasar de Gallegos sat on the back of his wildly prancing and snorting *sogwili*.

" 'Where is that God-damned Juan José,' he shouted.

"I ran toward him, my heart pounding from a confusion of emotions: fear and loathing, revulsion and anger.

" 'Here I am, Excellency,' I said. 'At your service, sir.'

" 'Talk to these people if you can,' he ordered. 'See if their chief is still among the living.'

"I approached near to one of the quivering captives, and Falda walked along beside me.

" 'Do you speak the trade language?' I asked.

"He looked at me stupidly. Perhaps he did not know it. Perhaps he was simply stunned senseless by the horror of what had just happened. I stepped to another and asked the same question and got basically the same response. Falda followed along, asking, I assumed, if they spoke her Timucua tongue. She got no better results than I did. After about six unsuccessful tries, I approached an old man.

" 'I can speak the jargon,' he said without waiting for my question. 'Who are you?'

" 'Like you,' I said, 'I'm a captive of these men. They made me their slave. I only do their bidding. I'm as horrified at their behavior as you are.'

" 'What do they want with us here?' he asked.

"I did not answer him. 'Is your chief alive?' I asked.

"He hesitated a moment, then looked toward a younger man standing to his right and behind him, and spoke to him in their native tongue. Not only could I not understand it, I did not recognize its sound. The younger man spoke back. Then the old man spoke to me again in the trade language.

" 'That man I just spoke to is our chief,' he said.

" 'Does he speak the jargon?'

" 'No.'

" 'Then I'll have to speak to him through you,' I said. I turned and walked back to Gallegos. 'There is their chief,' I said, 'over there, but I can speak to him only through the old man, the one I was talking with.'

" 'Bring them both forward then,' said the Español.

"I turned back toward the old man and spoke again in the jargon.

" 'Bring your chief and come forward,' I said. 'I don't like to speak to you in this manner, but that is what this man is telling me to say.'

"The old man spoke to his chief over his shoulder, and the two of them walked together to my side. The three of us stood waiting for further word from Gallegos. For a long time, he just stared, his face showing utter contempt.

"Finally, he spoke. 'Ask the chief,' he said, 'where he keeps his gold.'

"I put the question to the old man, who then spoke to his chief. The chief answered him briefly. The old man turned back to me.

" 'We have none of the yellow metal,' he said.

" 'They say they have none,' I told Gallegos.

" 'Then where will I find some? They must know that.'

"Again in the trade language I spoke to the old man.

" 'He wants to know where he can find the yellow metal,' I said. 'If you tell him something, perhaps he'll go away from here and leave you alone.'

"The old man and his chief had a brief discussion together, at the end of which the old man spoke one word.

" 'Cale,' he said.

" 'Cale?' I repeated.

" 'Is that the name of the place?' demanded Gallegos. 'Cale. Is that the place to find some gold?'

" 'That is what they said,' I answered.

" 'Tell the chief that I will need a guide to lead us there and twenty-eight *portadors* to carry our supplies. Tell him to select these men for me right away and line them up here.'

"I thought that I had seen the extent of the cruelty of these men, but it had only just begun. Twenty-nine strong young men were brought forward and lined up there before Gallegos. The one who was designated guide was removed from the line. He stood beside me and Falda. The others were all made to face in one direction, so that, except for the first in line, each man looked at the back of another.

"Then Gallegos called out to one of his men who came forward with his tools. Two others came with him bearing large, heavy bundles. They opened the bundles and brought out first twenty-eight heavy collars made of very hard metal. These they placed around the necks of the men they called their *portadors*. The collars were fastened in such a way that they could not be opened again.

"Then they brought out a long and heavy chain, a thing of the same metal as the collars, made of many links hooked together. It was like a rope or a braid, but it could not be broken, and it could not be cut. This chain they fastened to all of the collars, so that the twenty-eight men were all tied together in this manner.

"By the time all of this had been accomplished, it was late in the day. Gallegos declared that we would spend the night in Paracoxi. He had the arms of the chief bound behind his back, and each of the Español soldiers selected a house for himself for the night. They also selected for themselves young women of the town. My master, Capitán Viviano García, apparently having tired of Falda, selected a new one for himself as well.

"For a long time that night I was kept awake by the antics of García as well as the torments of my own thoughts. At some point in the night, my thoughts became dreams, but I still cannot tell where the separation was between the two. Part of the night my head entertained images of my early travels and my first captivity at the hands of the Fierce People. During that time I also thought about my traveling companions Water Moccasin and Like-a-Pumpkin.

"Then I thought or dreamed about my home, my family and friends. But most of the night, my mind was troubled with thoughts and images of the present times. I saw again and again the strange people who called themselves Españols, or *Cristianos*, chopping people to bits.

"Much of the night I wandered aimlessly in unknown country. I found myself dodging large, ferocious beasts. I endured again beatings I had suffered at the hands of my various captors. I listened to a babbling confusion of languages. But as bad as my night had been, I was not happy in the morning when I realized that it had come to an end, for I was afraid of what the new day would bring.

"The first sign of real trouble came when Gallegos learned that the man who had been designated guide had slipped away during the night. Gallegos went into a rage. He had the chief dragged before him in the middle of the town.

" 'Tell him,' he said, 'to explain this thing to me. Is this the way his subjects obey? To run away in the night? Tell him to explain.'

"We communicated in the same awkward manner as we had the day before, I speaking in the trade language to the old man, the old man speaking to his chief in the language of Paracoxi, then the process being reversed until I again spoke to Gallegos in his Español. In response to Gallegos's question, the chief said that the Españols had frightened the man so much that he had run away.

" 'Why have you put my young men in collars?' he asked. 'That is what frightened the man away. I want you to take the collars off these young men. They have already agreed to go with you and to help you carry your things. You don't need to keep them in collars the way you keep your animals. I want my young men released.'

"I shook with fear when I repeated those words in Español to Gallegos, and, as I suspected, his face turned red with anger as he listened. Then he roared his response.

" 'I will release you from your miserable life,' he said. Then he shouted to the men with the dogs. I could not believe what was happening right there before my eyes. I did not want to watch, but somehow I could not make myself close my eyes or turn my head away. Not at first.

"The men brought the snarling dogs forward. Then two men got hold of the chief and pushed him to the dogs. They attacked him the way a dog will attack a rabbit. They ripped at him with their sharp fangs. The chief screamed in horror as pieces of his flesh were ripped away. At last I managed to turn my head, and I covered my eyes with my hands. It was not possible, though, to block out the sounds of the growling, snarling, ripping and screaming.

"The contents of my stomach revolted. I dropped to my knees retching. It was a blessing, for I could no longer see or hear the terror that was taking place just behind me."

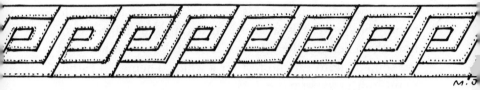

Eight

DEADWOOD LIGHTER seemed to falter. He put a hand to his forehead and staggered backward just a little. His old companion, Dancing Rabbit, was at his side quickly.

"Are you all right?" asked Dancing Rabbit. "What is it?"

"Yes. Yes. I'm all right. I felt weak for a moment. That's all. It will pass, and I'll go on with my story."

"Stop for a while," said Dancing Rabbit. "Rest. Have something to eat."

"The story must be told," said Deadwood Lighter.

"Yes, my friend. I agree with you about that, and for that reason you must keep your strength. Sit down now for a little while. Rest and eat. Then you can begin again."

The old man allowed himself to be ruled by Dancing Rabbit. He sat down, looking as if he lacked the strength to ever get up again. Dancing Rabbit then stood to address the crowd, which was absolutely silent, transfixed by the things they had just been told, hungering to hear more, at once frightened and thrilled by the horror of the tale being narrated. To all that had just been added a sudden apprehension for the well-being of the old man, the teller of the tale.

"Deadwood Lighter needs to rest," Dancing Rabbit told them. "So do we. His story is long and painful and tiring to both the teller and the listeners. Let's all go out of here and get something to eat and rest for a while. Then we'll gather again to hear some more."

No one moved at first. They seemed to lack the will. They sat as if stunned and uncertain. Dancing Rabbit moved to his sister's side and spoke closely into her ear.

"The old man needs some food," he said.

"I'll bring him some," she said. She got up to leave the townhouse, and then a few of the other people seemed to come out of their stupor. They stood to follow her out. Still they did not speak. They moved like shadows toward the door and on outside, quietly, almost reverently. They stared at the ground before them as they walked.

'Squani, though, still sat on the hard bench in the townhouse, still waited. He sat there alone, staring at the old man, this man who had been so long with the people of 'Squani's own mysterious and unknown father.

The tale of slaughter and slavery and greed he was hearing from the old man was horrible, yes, but it was also fascinating to the young half-breed. It was—it was his other half. He longed to see an Español—a *'squani.*

At last he stood up, and he almost walked over to the old man's side. Instead, after a slight hesitation, he headed for the door. After all, he thought, what would he have said?

The cool, crisp night air outside almost shocked him. It did send a sudden and uncontrollable shiver over his body. He stood for a few moments gulping down deep breaths of the clean, fresh air. It did his lungs good after having been for so long a time in the smoky interior of the townhouse.

His eyes still burned a little from all the smoke. He rubbed them with the backs of his hands. Then he started walking toward the house of his mother.

He found Potmaker standing in front of her house cooking small spitted cuts of venison over an open fire. 'Squani sat down on a tree stump just behind her and to her right. He leaned back against the front wall of the house and stared up at the sky. The smell of the cooking flesh and the warmth of the fire in the cool night were good.

"Are you hungry?" she asked him.

It seemed a long time before he answered. He had heard her, of course, but his mind was somewhere else, somewhere far off, trying to imagine the appearance of strange men he had heard described but had never seen, trying to envision the kinds of beasts these men could actually ride upon, trying to picture their clothing. He tried to remember the few words he had heard the old man speak in the language of these strange people who represented his other half: *Español, capitán, caballo.* There had been others, but he could not recall them.

But mostly his mind was on one particular unknown Español, his father. He knew that, even if he should somehow come face-to-face with the man, he would not know him. His mother did not even know who his father was. The father did not know, and if he had known, would not care.

'Squani knew the circumstances of his own conception. He had not been spared the tale. It had not been kept from him. He knew how his mother had been a captive of some Españols, and how several of them had used her to satisfy their lust. He longed to see his father, but he hated the man. Maybe he would at least get to see some Españols one of these days. What would he do when that time came? Would he go away with them and become one of them? Would he kill them? Would they kill him?

He was hungry, though, and slowly he shook himself loose from his troubling and confusing thoughts. "Yes, Mother," he said. "I am hungry."

"It will be ready soon," said Potmaker, smiling at him over her shoulder. She knew that he was troubled, and she knew the reasons. She understood as only a mother can understand her child. He was silent again, still staring into space, still, or again, lost in his own thoughts.

Carrier, his father, his adopted father, was not at the house. Likely he was with the men of his own mother's people, his own clan, the Wolf People. When Carrier had brought Potmaker, his Timucua wife, home with him from his final trip as a trader, they had not had a home. For among the Real People, the homes are owned by the women, and Potmaker was not one of the Real People.

But she had been welcomed, and Carrier's people had given her a spot to build in their midst so that she could have her own home, and then they had even helped her build her house there in Kituwah. But she did not belong to a clan, and, therefore, neither did her son.

So 'Squani did not quite think that he was himself a Real Person. True, he had been born among the Real People, had been raised among them as one of them and had never known a home other than his mother's house at Kituwah. He knew no ways other than the ways of the Real People, could speak no language but theirs.

But his mother had no clan. She was Timucua by birth and by raising. 'Squani knew almost nothing about the Timucuas. And if the Real People had truly accepted him, her child, as one of them, then why did they insist upon calling him 'Squani? He was, he thought bitterly, a *'squani*, and for that he hated his father, and by extension, he hated himself.

Suddenly 'Squani realized that his moping thoughts had been terribly selfish. He had been feeling sorry for himself in his confusion of thoughts, his puzzle of birth and raising. Listening to the story of the Españols had brought all the thoughts to the front of his mind, but what of his mother?

How could he not have thought of her? What memories must the old man's stories of the Españols have forced her to relive? And what new worries for old friends and relatives must be now in her mind? The Timucuas were her people. The land that had been decimated by these Españols in the tales that Deadwood Lighter had been telling, that was her land. He looked at her again, trying now to read the pain that he knew she must be feeling, but if it was there inside her, she did not betray it. She kept it close, hidden, secret. She was, he realized for the first time in his life, a strong woman, and all at once he admired her tremendously.

"Mother," he said, "are you all right?"

For a moment, she kept working, looking straight ahead. Then she stopped and stared ahead in silence. At last she turned to face her son. She gave him an understanding smile.

"Here in Kituwah among the Real People, this is my home now," she said, "and my life is here, but that was my home. My life began in that place as a Timucua woman, and I hurt for the people there. But, yes, my son, I'm all right. It's you I worry for now."

Back in the townhouse, Deadwood Lighter sipped the last of the bowl of stew that Sedi, Walnut, had brought to him. It tasted good. It tasted like real food should taste, not like the food the Españols had given him to eat. It was good to be home among the people who were, or at least had been, his own people.

But home had changed during his long absence. Men's Town was gone, and with it, the ruling class of priests, the ancient *Ani-Kutani*. It was difficult to imagine even how the *Ani-yunwi-ya*, the Real People, could continue to exist without the constant guidance of the *Ani-Kutani*. The priests had been in charge of all of the ancient rituals that kept the earth in balance.

Ah, he thought, as if by sudden revelation. Perhaps that explains everything. The people rose up against the *Ani-Kutani* and killed them all, and now the Españols are destroying the land and the people and everything else around. The world is truly out of balance.

So many things had changed. The world of the Real People that Deadwood Lighter remembered from earlier years no longer existed. Men's Town was gone. The *Ani-Kutani* were no more. There was no semblance of central authority left among the Real People. None. Each town had become autonomous.

And there were even new words in the language: *sogwili* and *Ani-Asquani*. These were, of course, results of the intrusion of the Españols into the country. There would be more, for the Españols had brought other new and strange things with them for which words would have to be found. But new words in the language would be the least of the changes the Real People would have to face, he thought.

He wondered what the future would hold for them, for his people. Of course, they had brought it on themselves, whatever it might be, when they had killed the priests. Yet still he worried for them. He felt toward them the way a mother or maternal uncle might feel toward a child that had misbehaved. He felt at once like scolding them for their unruly behavior and protecting them from danger, whether from themselves or from outside forces.

The De Soto expedition was gone, and De Soto himself was dead, but there would be more like him. Of that Deadwood Lighter was certain. There were so many of those Españols. And, he thought, they keep coming in those big ships. I myself will probably never see another one. I won't live that long. But they will be back. They will. They or some of the others.

Deadwood Lighter had heard the Españols talk about the *Francés*, the *Portugués* and the *Inglés*. He had never seen any of these people, but he had understood that they were, like the Españols, white people from across the sea. They spoke different languages, and they were enemies of the Españols, but from what Deadwood Lighter had been able to understand about them, in spite of the fact that the Españols cursed them, they were really all of them very much alike.

Like the Españols, they were traveling around the world in ships, looking for gold, making slaves of people, killing and taking land. Like the Españols, they seemed to think that they should be the rulers of the whole earth. Sooner or later, they would come to the land of the Real People. What would it be like then? he wondered.

There were so many questions, for which he did not know the answers. He was afraid for his people, for their future. And he was old and tired. He was old beyond his years. He did not have much more time. He knew that. He would not be around much longer to give them help or advice.

There was but one thing left he could do for them. He could finish the story to let them know what the white men were like, to impress upon them the possible extent of the horror, and the tale would be a warning and a lesson to them to be prepared for what was almost certain to come. That was all that he could do. It was all that he would have time for.

He had already put down the bowl. He waved a feeble arm in a gesture to Dancing Rabbit to come back to his side. His former companion hurried to respond.

"My old friend," said Deadwood Lighter, touching the other former *Kutani* lightly on the arm, "I'm rested. I'm much better now. Bring the people back in here. The tale must go on."

Nine

ALL OVER TOWN the story, so far as it had gone, was being retold. People who had not been able to get inside the townhouse or even close enough to the door to hear were asking others to tell them what had been said. Some others were simply repeating to each other parts of the tale that they had all heard.

"Where can these people have come from?" someone asked.

"Across the waters, they say."

"What can it be about them that makes them so cruel?"

"Their greed for the yellow metal."

"I think that they are a whole race of crazy people."

"I think you may be right."

"Do you think maybe this old man, this Deadwood Lighter, is crazy? Maybe his story is not true."

"I think his story is true. We've heard rumors enough about these *Ani-'squani* before. Now we're hearing from someone who was actually with them for a long time."

"Yes. Remember, Carrier and his Timucua woman fought

against these same people. The way this old man tells it, it's just like what they told."

"Yes. Except he was with them for a long time and has even more to tell."

"I think I know why these men are so crazy."

"Tell us why then."

"They have no women. Have you ever heard any mention from anybody about *Ani-Asquani* women? I have not. There are only men. They're running around the world trying to catch the women of other people. That's what makes them so crazy."

"If they have no women, how is it then that they have not vanished?"

"They catch the women of others and make little *'squanis.*"

"Like our own 'Squani?"

Then there was some laughter, although it was not raucous. The general mood was too tense for that. Then a man came running toward the group.

"Dancing Rabbit is calling us back into the townhouse," he said. "The old man is ready to start telling his tale again."

"Come on then. Let's go. We won't be able to get a place for ourselves."

Soon they were gathered again. Some of the ones who had been left out before managed to get inside, and some who had been in were left out. They were murmuring as they settled down to their places, but when Deadwood Lighter stood, still leaning on the broken lance, a hush descended upon the crowd.

"Well," began Deadwood Lighter, "we left that town. We left it desolate and sad. We left it in mourning. We left it without a chief. We left behind us a trail of blood, and we took with us twenty-eight young men in chains. We were looking for the place called Cale, the place where they had said we would find the yellow metal.

"We were led by Gallegos. My master García and I and Falda were still together. The governor, De Soto, with many of his men and all of his *sikwas*, was still back at his main camp near the big water, not far from his big boats.

"For the next several days we passed through a number of small towns without incident. The people were spared, I think, by the haste of Gallegos to find Cale. We paused at each place just long enough to eat and to ask directions. Always the people told us that Cale was farther to the north. We kept going.

"At last we were told that not too far ahead of us was a place called Acela or maybe Vicela. It was a large town, and it was not far from Cale. Gallegos sent a man riding a *sogwili* back to inform De Soto and to give him directions to this place. He said that we would wait there.

"That night we spent on a dry plain. It was a hot night, and the Españols suffered greatly from the heat. I would have been glad of that, except that in their suffering they became even more mean-spirited than usual. I noticed, too, that night, that some of the men in collars and chains had become ill. That did not seem to bother the Españols, though.

"We had now been in the land the Españols called Florida for a full moon, and it was the moon of *guye quoni*, the moon when the corn is in tassel. The Españols called it *Julio*. And they called the year by a number, and the number was 1539.

"Five days later we arrived at the town called Acela, and the governor was there before us. I could not decide whether or not I was pleased to have him there in charge again. I was certainly glad that Gallegos was no longer in charge. But really, one was as bad as the other.

"At Acela two of the men in chains died from their illness, and then I witnessed for the first time another of the casual horrors of these men. The heavy collars and chains were of more value to them than were the bodies of the dead.

"They calmly cut off the heads of the dead men in order to remove them from the chain. I was disgusted, revolted, but I no longer became ill when I witnessed their bloody deeds. I was becoming hardened, like a callus on the skin, and that realization made me worry for the state of my own spirit.

"We did not stay long at Acela, for De Soto, like Gallegos, was anxious to find Cale and the yellow metal. We pushed on. The Españols still suffered from the heat, yet they did not remove their heavy clothing. It made them stink, for they did not bathe regularly either, as we do.

"I was particularly pleased then when we reached a large lake, and De Soto declared that we would camp there. It was a hot day, and the nasty Españols actually removed their clothing and went into the lake to bathe. That was a great, though temporary, relief.

"We stayed for two days and nights at this lake, and the reason was that De Soto was waiting for the rest of his men to arrive, those who were driving the herd of *sikwas*. Toward the end of the second day, they arrived. I heard one of the Españols say, 'Now perhaps we'll have some meat to eat.' But none of the *sikwas* were killed.

"Watching the poor men trying to manage such a large herd of animals, I was again glad that I had been spared that assignment. The *sikwas* squealed and snorted, and though the main herd stayed bunched more or less together, some were always straying away and running off in all directions.

The men shouted and chased them, and the brutal big dogs barked ferociously and jerked at their leashes. The soldiers enjoyed this spectacle and laughed loudly at the poor herdsmen.

"We abandoned our camp by the lake and traveled for another day, at the end of which we found ourselves beside a swollen river. The Españols called it a swamp. While we were there some of the men rode out to search for signs of life. They returned with a captive. Juan Ortiz was able to converse with the man, so he must have been a Timucua, or from some people closely related to the Timucuas. He called the river there by the name of Ocale, and he said that the whole region around us was called Ocale and consisted of several villages. The nearest was within a day's walk of us.

"De Soto and the other Españols became very excited, for they thought that Ocale might be the same place that they had been told about by the name of Cale, the place where they would find the yellow metal.

"We slept there by the River Ocale that night, and the next day we traveled to the village. It was called Uqueten, and it was the first village of Ocale. We stayed there for fifteen days.

"As before at the other places, De Soto took over the village as if he were master of the world. He took the town chief captive, keeping him near himself at all times and threatening to kill him if the people of the village failed to obey his every order.

"He took some new *portadors* from among the population of Uqueten to replace those who had died, and he had the heavy collars placed around their necks. The Españols made the people of Uqueten feed them, and they made casual use of the young women there.

"There was no yellow metal to be seen anywhere in the

village, and the chief and the people there claimed to have none. My master Viviano García and I were present when De Soto angrily questioned the chief.

" 'I was told that I would find gold at Cale,' he said. 'Is there another place called by that name? I think that I am being lied to, and that makes me very angry. Perhaps if I feed some of your people to my dogs, your tongue will loosen.'

" 'Ocale is a very large place,' said the chief. 'Uqueten is but one small town within Ocale. Here in the southern part of Ocale, we are poor. The richer towns are to the north. The town you are looking for is called Uzachil. It's our northernmost town, and it's the place where our principal chief resides. He keeps all of the riches, all of the yellow metal, there at Uzachil.'

" 'Good,' said the governor. 'Then you will take me there.'

"It was the moon of *galoni*, the end of the fruit, called by the Españols *Agosto*, when we left the village of Uqueten. The chief and fifteen other men of the village went with us. De Soto kept the chief beside him all the time. The others were used as *portadors* and carried heavy burdens as they walked along.

" 'Do you believe, Juan José,' my master asked me as I walked along beside him, 'that we will find gold at Uzachil?'

" 'I don't know, *Capitán*,' I said. 'I have never seen this Uzachil. I know nothing about it.'

" 'Well, we had better,' he said. 'If we don't, this chief will surely die. And many others too.'

"Before the end of our first day out of Uqueten, we arrived at another village, but we passed through it with almost no incidents. The chief of Uqueten had already convinced De Soto that he would find nothing of value until we reached Uzachil.

"The next four days, we traveled through a village each day. The Españols left all of them almost the way they found them. De Soto was in a great hurry to reach Uzachil.

"Then we stopped at a fair-sized town which was called something like Cholupaha. It was beside a river, and the chief of Uqueten said that we would have to cross the river to reach Uzachil. De Soto decided that we would rest awhile at Cholupaha.

"As always, each Español moved into a house, putting out its rightful occupants. Most of them took for themselves one of the young women of the village. The villagers were made to provide and prepare food to feed the ravenous soldiers, as well as to provide grain for the *sogwilis*. The men with the herd of *sikwas* would be along later, for they were unable to keep up with us.

"A few more of the *portadors* had died or been killed by Españols, so De Soto took young men from Cholupaha to replace them.

"We slept the first night at Cholupaha, and the next day the Españols spent in building a bridge across the river, for it was deep and fast-running, and they were afraid to try to cross it any other way. They felled great trees and trimmed the trunks and lashed them together until they had spanned the river. Much of the labor, of course, was accomplished by the young men of Cholupaha, under the supervision of the Españols. The work took all of the day, and we slept a second night there in the town.

"The next day the herdsmen arrived with the squealing *sikwas*, and we spent that day crossing the River of Discords, the name the Españols had given to the swift river there. It took all day long to get all of the people and all of the animals across. We slept that night on the ground in the open country. The next day we traveled to another small village, a place called Caliquen.

"The governor was ready for another rest by that time, and so we settled in at Caliquen in the same manner as at the other places. Caliquen was also on a river, and the Españols called it Agua Caliquen, meaning in their language Caliquen Water.

"My master told me that one of the reasons for the long and frequent stops was to allow the *sogwilis* to rest and eat and regain their strength.

" 'Otherwise we would ride them to death,' he said, 'and then where would we be? Without our *caballos* we would die in this wilderness.'

"I wondered how he thought that the people who lived there had managed to survive for so long without the benefit of beasts to ride upon, but I kept my thought to myself. Most of my thoughts were best kept to myself.

"We stayed at this place for about twenty days, I think, and then, I suppose, the animals were fat enough again. I think that there could have been no virgins left in Caliquen by then and not much food. A few young men were taken to replace dead *portadors*. The chief was not taken captive nor was he killed. That was, I think, because De Soto still had the chief of Uqueten as his hostage.

"We crossed the river Agua Caliquen without a bridge, for it was not too deep or swift. Once again we were traveling. It was now the moon of *dulisdi*, nut, which the Españols called *Septiembre*. We reached a village that night, but there were no people there. It had been abandoned.

" 'Why are there no people in this place?' my master asked me.

" 'In these parts,' I told him, 'it's a common practice to

leave a village every few years and build a new one some distance away. It's because of the gardens.'

"What I had told him was true, of course, as all of you know, but what I did not tell him was that I did not believe that was the reason this particular village had been abandoned. I believed that the people had known that we were coming, and that was the reason they had left. We stayed in the abandoned village that night.

"We traveled for two days before finding another village. It too was abandoned, and we stayed there for a night. Then we traveled for three days to yet another one.

"This empty village was beside a swamp. After we had settled in for the night, the fifteen men still with us from the village of Uqueten asked to speak to De Soto. He allowed them to do so, and they begged him to release their chief, promising that if he did, they would stay with him and obey him and not attempt to escape.

" 'I need him with me,' said the governor, 'to lead me to Uzachil. Do as I say and give me no trouble, and I will release him at Uzachil.'

" 'Do you think that he will release their chief at Uzachil?' I asked my master in a low voice.

" 'Ha,' said García. 'One never knows. He may. He may release his soul from his unworthy body.'

M·J·

Ten

I DON'T KNOW how or why, but I slept well that night. I slept like a baby. We three, García and Falda and I, shared a small house toward the center of the town. After I got used to the not-too-distant sounds of the animals, the night seemed amazingly quiet. I think that De Soto's men were tired, and even they welcomed a night in a quiet, abandoned village. It was still warm, but not so hot and sultry as it had been before. I don't even remember dreaming that night. I only recall waking up abruptly, frightened out of a deep sleep.

"It was just dawn when the shrieks awoke me. Even though it was an abrupt awakening, I recognized the sounds immediately for what they were: the war cries of hundreds of angry voices. At that moment, I knew where all of the young men from the abandoned villages had gone. I knew why they had abandoned their homes and what they had been planning.

"García was up from his cot in an instant, his sword in his right hand. He ran wildly out of the house. I moved quickly to the doorway to look out and see what was happening. Falda was by my side. Both of us were trembling from fright. The attackers seemed to be everywhere, and their shrieks were hideous. Españols were coming out of all the houses, armed to defend themselves. The fighting which followed was ferocious.

"I saw my master with one mighty swipe of his sword almost take the head off an attacker. I saw an arrow come out of the sky to bury itself in the chest of one Español, and I rejoiced in that small victory. I heard screams of agony in the midst of the other sounds of battle.

"For a few moments I had hopes that the cruel Españols would be defeated, but then some of them got to their *sogwilis*, and when they raced into the midst of the attackers on the backs of those huge beasts, the tide of the battle turned. Soon the attackers were routed. They ran from the village in all directions.

"The Españols chased after them, but many of them ran into large ponds at the fringes of the swamp to escape. The Españols did not follow them into the water. I don't know why. Perhaps they could not swim. Perhaps they feared something in the water. I remember that I had heard them call it a bad swamp. Anyway, the battle was over as quickly as it had begun. De Soto stomped about the village angrily. His ugly red face looked as if it might burst open in his rage.

" 'Gallegos,' he cried. 'Come to me. Gallegos.'

"Almost immediately, Baltasar de Gallegos appeared by his side. He held a sword which was dripping with blood, and his own body was spattered red almost from head to toe.

" 'Get some mounted men and pursue the bastards,' De Soto said. 'Catch them alive if you can. Kill them if you must, but allow none to escape.'

"Gallegos ran off to do his governor's bidding, and De

Soto stalked around some more. By this time, Falda and I had ventured a little way out of the house in which we had been lurking. We stayed close together, though, and close to the house. My master García came walking toward us, but before he could get to us, the governor saw him.

" 'García,' he said. 'What are the casualties? Do you know?'

" 'We have only one dead, Excellency,' said García. 'Several were wounded, but none too badly, I think. One horse is hurt. I've not checked the pigs.'

" 'Never mind all that,' said De Soto. 'How many enemy killed?'

" 'There are thirty-eight bodies of the attacking *Indios* lying about in the village,' said García, 'and four *portadors* who revolted and tried to help the attackers were also killed.'

" 'How many *Indios* do you think were in the attacking force, García?'

" 'I estimate well over three hundred, Governor. Perhaps as many as four hundred.'

" 'Yes. Yes,' said the governor. 'Four hundred. By God, it was a good fight. A great victory. Take over here, García. See that everything is under control. I'm going to get dressed now. Take command.'

" 'Juan José,' called García. I ran to him at once, Falda tagging along behind me.

" '*Sí, mi capitán?*'

" 'Go check on the governor's swine and report back to me,' he said. Then he added in a low voice, 'There's no need to hurry.'

"The large herd of *sikwas* was outside of the village near the edge of the swamp. I started walking in that direction, and Falda walked along beside me. I heard her sigh heavily.

" 'I guess no one can beat them,' she said, 'these white men from across the sea.'

"I put an arm around her shoulders and pulled her close to my side as we walked along, and I realized that both of us were still trembling. I felt like a father—or a grandfather— trying to comfort a child.

" 'It seems so,' I said.

" 'Will they kill us all before they are through?'

" 'I don't know. But I seem to recall an old prophecy. It told of the coming of white men from across the waters. It said that they would steal the land and almost ruin it. It said that they would try to wipe out the People and would nearly succeed, but at last they would go back where they came from.'

" 'I hope that I'm still alive to see the end of the prophecy come about,' said Falda.

" 'Yes,' I said. 'I hope you are too.'

"We walked on toward the place where the *sikwas* were being kept, and then I saw some of the mounted men returning. Some were driving captives ahead of them. Others were leading or dragging their captives along behind them by long ropes.

"We saw one Español come riding back into the village with a lead rope. He was riding fast. Behind him, a captive, his wrists tied together, was running to keep up. Suddenly the rider kicked his beast in its sides, causing it to jump and race ahead even faster. The captive behind was jerked off his feet. He yelled as he flew through the air. Then he landed on his belly and was dragged. I turned my face away.

" 'Don't look,' I said to Falda. We walked on toward the *sikwas*. As we got closer to them, the smell of the herd became horribly oppressive. Once again I felt some pity for the herdsmen and was glad that I was not one of them. Then the herdsman nearest us, looking over his shoulder for a moment, saw us coming. I hailed him with a gesture, and he turned to walk toward us. We met halfway. I was thankful that he did not make us walk any closer to the foul-smelling and unruly herd.

" 'My master, Capitán Viviano García, sent me to find out about the *puercos*,' I said in the language of the Españols. 'Were any hurt or lost during the battle?'

" 'We lose some every day,' the man said. 'I don't know how many. How could anyone count these swine? We're chasing them all the time, trying to keep them together. It's madness trying to travel through this country with this many pigs. And why? What are they for? Have we had pork to eat? No. How many pigs were lost? How should I or anyone know? Tell García— Tell him that everything is all right here. I don't think we lost any more during the battle than we would have lost without it. Tell him the pigs are doing just fine.'

"Just then a large *sikwa* ran snorting and snuffling from the herd, headed toward the village, and we were between it and the village. I believe that my startled expression alerted the man with whom I was speaking. He turned to look over his shoulder and saw it coming toward us.

" *'Perdón,'* he said, and he ran for the beast, waving the short staff he carried in his right arm. The *sikwa* saw him coming and tried to stop and change its direction, but the man came up close in front of it. Then he yelled at it and swung his staff and struck the animal on its short snout with a loud smack. The *sikwa* squealed out in pain, turned and ran back to the seeming safety of the herd.

" 'Let's go back now,' I said to Falda. She turned with me, and we started walking back toward the village. More horsemen were coming in, bringing more captives, many of whom were wounded. Back in the center of the village, Españols were lining up the captives as they came in. Some of them were bound, some were not. Behind the line, Españols held on leashes the snarling big dogs. Juan Ortiz was questioning the prisoners one after another. The governor, having dressed himself, looked on sternly. Falda and I spotted García and walked over to stand by him.

" *'Los puercos son seguros,'* I said.

" *'Bueno,'* said García. 'Now stand close by. We may need you for interpreters if Ortiz is not able to do the job here.'

" *'Sí, señor,'* I said, but Ortiz seemed to me to be doing a good enough job. Apparently the governor agreed with me on that, for I was not called upon to help, nor was Falda.

"For a little while I was not able to tell just what was going on, but soon Ortiz had moved far enough down the line for me to hear. I did not understand what he was saying to the captives, but Falda could. I whispered to her in the trade jargon.

" 'What is he trying to find out?' I asked.

" 'He's trying to identify their leaders,' she said.

"Now and then Ortiz turned away from the line of captives to speak to De Soto. Then his process of questioning the captives would continue. The rest of the morning and much of the afternoon was taken up in this manner, and by the time poor Ortiz was allowed to rest from his labor, he had interviewed nearly two hundred captives. Twelve of them were taken apart from the rest.

" 'Bring collars and chains for these dozen chiefs,' said De Soto. 'They'll soon learn that an *Indio* chief is nothing but a slave to me.'

"The heavy collars were fastened around the necks of the twelve men who had been identified as the chiefs or leaders of the attack. They were also said to be the chiefs of the towns we had found abandoned. The chain was fastened to each of the collars. Then De Soto walked out to stand in front of the remaining captives, now a little less than two hundred.

" 'Tell them that these are their chiefs,' he said, 'these men standing here before them in irons. Tell them that they have been fools to follow these men. Tell them that they are about to die for their chiefs.'

"Juan Ortiz spoke out loud to the group gathered there, and then he stepped aside. De Soto gave a nod to Gallegos, who whipped out his sword and ran it through the middle of the captive nearest to him. Other Españols followed his example. They stabbed, and they hacked. Their victims were all unarmed, all naked. Many of them were already hurt and bleeding.

"Some few tried to run, but they were cut down after only a few steps. It seemed to me that blood was spurting through the air, and before they were done with their evil work, all of the executioners were covered with the blood of their victims. Falda had hidden her face on my chest, but I watched the entire process with a terrible fascination.

"Then the screams stopped. The hacking and chopping and stabbing stopped. The bloody bodies on the ground were still. Only their blood ran, soaking the ground beneath and around them. Only the stench of death rose up from their remains.

"The killers stood panting for breath, for they had nearly exhausted themselves in their fervor. I stole a glance at my master García and thought that I could detect a little disgust, perhaps even disapproval, on his face. For a brief moment, then, I wondered if it might be possible that among these monsters were a few human beings.

"There was a long quiet. No one spoke. No one moved, except De Soto. He paced along in front of the butchered bodies there on the red-stained ground in front of him.

" 'Let loose the dogs,' he said. 'In the morning, first thing, we go on to Uzachil.'

Eleven

I T WAS ABOUT EIGHT DAYS later when we stopped at a place to camp for the night beside a river called the River of the Deer. After a time spent in searching the banks and several attempts by individuals to cross, it was determined that the river was too deep and swift for a crossing. De Soto decided that another bridge would be built.

"Uzachil, with its yellow metal, he had been told, was on the other side, and the governor was determined to go to Uzachil. Gallegos was placed in charge of the bridge-building project, and for the next two days, he worked the men very hard. Some of the poor *portadors*, I thought, seemed ready to fall over and die. The Españols, of course, seemed not in the least concerned about the condition of those *Indios*.

"The process used here was much the same as before. Large trees were felled and trimmed of their branches. They were then lashed together in order to span the river. The hard labor required to accomplish this task was made all the more difficult by the fact that there was not enough food to eat, and the Españols fed themselves first. The *Indios* starved as they worked.

"I myself felt weak from hunger, and I was not required to work on the bridge. I think that some of the Españols felt that I was being pampered unnecessarily and resented that very much, but my master García was extremely possessive and would have no one but himself ordering me about. For that quirk of his personality I was most grateful.

"When the work was finally done, we crossed the river without much incident. The most excitement occurred when the herdsmen began driving the *sikwas* across the bridge. I think that the Españols would have liked to stay and watch and laugh at the spectacle, but De Soto was almost mad in his desire to reach Uzachil. We left the *sikwas* and their drovers to catch up with us the best they could.

"Again we passed through several small deserted villages, and at last, the captive chief told De Soto that the next town ahead was Uzachil. De Soto pressed us on harder than ever. When the *portadors* failed to walk as fast as the Españols wanted them to go, men on the backs of *sogwilis* lashed at them with long whips, cutting their backs, sometimes to the bone. When they fell under their heavy burdens, too weak to rise again, they were quickly killed and their heads cut off to free the bodies from the long chain.

"We had lived so long with horrible brutalities that I discovered my emotions were almost numb. I casually noted when the Españols casually killed. I remember thinking that if I did not find a way to escape from these men, I, myself, would soon become less than human, as much a monster as they. At times, I was afraid that I had already done so.

"Then, suddenly it seemed, we had reached our goal. Uzachil. We heard someone cry it out from the head of the column. 'Uzachil!' Falda and I exchanged a glance.

" 'If he finds the yellow metal here,' she said to me, 'do you think he will then go away?'

" 'I don't know, Falda,' I said. 'Sometimes I feel that I will die marching along with these Españols. I don't know what he will do if he finds it. I think that I know, though, what he will do if he fails to find it.'

"The day was coming to a close as we marched down into Uzachil, and it quickly became clear to us that once again, word of our approach had preceded us. Uzachil had been completely abandoned. There were a few stray dogs, but there were no people.

"I fully expected to be subjected to watching another of De Soto's rages, but he was remarkably calm. He held up a hand to halt the column behind him, and then he rode slowly into the village, looking first to his right, then to his left. A dog barked at him as he approached it, but when the strange, big four-legged beast got close to it, the dog turned and ran away. When the governor reached the center of the village, he stopped, turned around and rode back to his place at the head of the column.

" 'Gallegos,' he said, 'search the town, and kill the dogs.'

" 'Yes, Governor,' said Gallegos. He turned and waved an arm and several others followed him. The rest of us waited where we were. I don't know about the others, but I was terribly nervous, still waiting for the governor's temper to explode. It did not. In a few moments, Gallegos returned. I think he had not killed the dogs. I think they ran away as he and the others rode through the town.

" 'There is no one here,' he said.

" 'Food?' said De Soto.

" 'We found large stores of maize and beans and pumpkins,' said Gallegos.

" 'Good,' said De Soto. 'We'll stop here for the night.

Perhaps even for a few days. The men and horses will be well
fed by the time we're ready to leave. By the way, Gallegos.
You know what it means that you have found so much food
here, don't you? So much food and no *Indios?*'

" 'Why, no, Governor,' said Gallegos. 'I don't know what
that means.'

" 'It means that this town, like the others, has not been
moved. It means that this town was abandoned recently, just
because the *Indios* knew we were coming. Get everyone settled in, Gallegos. We'll talk some more later.'

"And so we feasted that night on the stores of food from
the village of Uzachil. Everyone was remarkably quiet, probably because of the strange mood that the governor was in.
As usual we slept in the houses of the village that night. The
next morning, De Soto sent out his search parties, as he had
done before in other places.

"As the day progressed, the mounted men came in from
time to time with prisoners. By evening, they had captured
one hundred, and, again as usual, De Soto had them put
immediately in collars and chains. Again we ate from the
local stores, and then we spent a second night at Uzachil. De
Soto was still calm.

"In the morning, the captives from Uzachil were lined up
in the center of the village in front of the townhouse for
questioning. The questioner was again Juan Ortiz. I watched
as before, with Falda by my side. Neither of us was asked to
participate, so I had to gather what I could from the conversation which took place between the governor and Ortiz.

"He was, of course, asking them about the yellow metal.
They told him that they had none. In spite of this, and in
spite of the fact that his searches had turned up no sign of
the yellow metal, De Soto insisted that there was yellow
metal hidden somewhere at Uzachil.

"At last, his patience at an end, the governor had one of the captives tortured. I turned my head away. Even with all I had seen, I could not watch. But I heard the screams. There was no way to shut them out of my ears. The poor man died proclaiming what I believe to have been the truth—that there was no yellow metal in Uzachil.

"Calmly, De Soto turned to Juan Ortiz.

" 'Do you believe him?' he asked.

" '*Sí*, Governor. I do.'

"The governor then turned to Gallegos, who was standing there by his side.

" 'Gallegos,' he said, 'do you think that the man told the truth?'

" '*Sí*,' said Gallegos. 'If there was gold here, he would have told us rather than suffer the torture. He would not have died with a lie on his lips when the truth would have saved his life.'

" 'The truth would not have saved his life,' said De Soto, 'although he, of course, did not know that.'

"He turned and walked away from Gallegos a few paces, then spoke to him again without even bothering to look back over his shoulder.

" 'Well then,' he said, 'kill the lying chief that led us here.'

"Gallegos drew out his long sword, and again I looked away. I felt a scream deep inside of me that wanted to burst out. Would I die in the midst of this brutality? Would I ever be free of these monsters from across the sea? How much more would I witness? And why?

"Toward evening of that day, the men driving the great herd of *sikwas* arrived and shattered the relative calm that had set in. Some of the animals broke loose from the herd and ran squealing through the village. Men ran after them with their long staffs, shouting and cursing. Eventually they got them all back together again. At least that's what they told the governor.

"I overheard one Español say to another, 'I don't know why we have to eat like horses with all that pork right there.'

"We slept another night at Uzachil.

"In the morning it was discovered that six of the recent captives had escaped in the night, killing their guards. The Españols were found strangled to death by their own chains. I saw one of the bodies. The face was blue and puffy, and the tongue was purple and sticking out of the mouth. Secretly, I rejoiced at the sight until I saw what the governor was going to do in retaliation. He had twenty-four of the remaining captives slain in front of us all. He would have killed more, I am sure, but he needed them for *portadors* and for grinders of corn, so many had already died from hunger, overwork and harsh treatment.

"Then, the killing done, suddenly, brusquely, he ordered us to pack up. We left Uzachil behind us in flames.

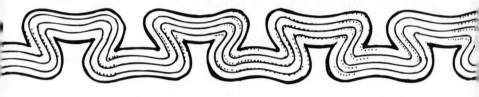

Twelve

W E TRAVELED four days, leaving the herdsmen and the *sikwas* behind to struggle along at their own slow pace, and we passed a high forest and came to a pine wood. Then we came to a small village which was called Agile, and this place was inhabited by a people who were allied to the Apalachees, though there were none at home there in the village but a few very old ones.

"De Soto soon discovered that Juan Ortiz could no longer serve as interpreter, for he did not know the language of these people. So once again, I was called upon to make use of my skills. I did not know the language either, but I tried the trade language and found that several of the old men there could speak it.

"They freely admitted that their town was all but deserted because they had known of De Soto's approach. When asked why they had not run away with the others, one of the old men grinned a wide and almost toothless grin.

" 'None of us here run so well anymore,' he said, 'and

besides, to lose our lives would not be much loss. They are almost over already.'

"The other old men chuckled, but De Soto scowled at the answer. He had Gallegos steal some corn and beans, and then we went on our way. He left the old men alive and unharmed, and I said a secret, silent prayer of thanks for that small favor.

"The next day we came to a river with swampy banks. As we drew nearer, we could see that a man was standing there near the swamp. He looked as if he might be just waiting for us to arrive. He stood facing us, hands on his hips. De Soto held up his hand to stop us. We were still a good bow shot away from the man.

" 'Capitán García,' said the governor, 'take your talking slave over there and find out who that savage is and what he's doing there.'

"We went to the man, my master and I, he riding on the back of his beast, I trotting along beside. Falda waited behind for us with the others. As soon as we were close enough to hear, the man spoke. He greeted us in the trade language.

" 'Who are you?' I asked him. 'And what are you doing here?'

" 'I'm a messenger from my chief, the mighty Vitachuco,' he said. 'He sent me here to meet you and to lead you on in to Ivitachuco.'

"I took it that the extra sound placed in front of the chief's name had the meaning of something like place. I translated for García, and then I stayed there with Vitachuco's messenger while my master rode back to tell De Soto what the man had said.

" 'You are not one of them,' the messenger said to me.

" 'No,' I answered. 'Long ago I was captured by people to

the far west and made a slave. They sold me to these Españols. The one who rode up here to speak with you is my
master.'

"The messenger looked as if he would speak to me again,
but just then De Soto moved, and his entire column moved
along behind him. He rode right up to where I was standing
with the messenger, so close as to seem menacing, especially
from high up on the back of his snorting and stamping
sogwili, but the bold messenger did not flinch.

" 'Juan José,' said De Soto, calling me by the name my
master had given me, 'is this a trap, do you think?'

"I did not know what to say. I looked at the messenger.
He was not afraid. He stood there, in fact, just a bit arrogant,
I thought, almost defiant. I glanced at my master García and
then I looked back at De Soto. I shrugged.

" 'I don't know, Excellency,' I said.

" 'Of course you don't know, you blubbering ass,' he said.
'I asked you what you think.'

" 'But Excellency,' I said, 'I really don't know what to
think. May I question the man further?'

" 'Do,' said the governor with a sneer, 'please.'

"I turned back to the messenger, and I tried to look stern.
I'm afraid, though, that I must have failed miserably in the
attempt. I was tired, weak and worn. I probably seemed old
and afraid.

" 'Why is it,' I said, 'that this Vitachuco has sent you out
here to meet us and to lead us into his town when almost all
others along the way abandon their villages and fly into the
forest in fear before we arrive? Why is that?'

" 'Those others are cowards,' said the man. 'They are
afraid of your masters, and they are also afraid of my chief.
Vitachuco fears no one. He's the most powerful chief in

these parts. Those others you speak of, they all pay tribute to Vitachuco.'

" 'But why are you here? What does your chief want of us?' I asked.

" 'Only to meet these people you travel with,' answered the messenger. 'He has never seen any of their kind. He has heard of them and would like to meet them. He has had a great feast prepared with which to welcome them to his land. Ivitachuco is just across the river. Not far from here. Will you follow me?'

"I translated for the governor, and then I said, 'I do not believe it's a trap. I believe the man is delivering the message Vitachuco sent, and I believe that Vitachuco is sincere. It's the custom around here for a local powerful chief to welcome a visiting powerful chief in such a manner. Apparently, Excellency, Vitachuco is the most powerful chief around.'

"I did believe that, too, and still, after all that has happened, I believe it. Had Vitachuco meant to lay a trap, I think, he would not have sent so bold a messenger. I think that he was curious about the Españols. He had heard of their brutal conquests, but he was not afraid.

"Vitachuco, I believe, was a man of supreme confidence in himself and in his warriors. In addition, I think that Vitachuco probably thought that the Españols would possibly make valuable allies, both for purposes of trade and for military purposes against his enemies.

" 'Well then,' said De Soto, 'tell the man to lead us on. Lead on to— What is the name of his town?'

" 'Ivitachuco,' I said. 'Vitachuco's place.'

"The messenger, who had become our guide, was true to his word. We were in Vitachuco's town before the Sun had gone down to the bottom of the Sky Vault in the west. We were greeted by the local villagers as if we had been welcome and expected guests, and I suppose, in a way, we were. It was a great change and a real pleasure, but of course, it was not to last.

" 'These people actually seem happy to see us,' Falda said to me in the trade language, and there was amazement in her face and in her voice.

" 'They do not know what these men are like,' I said, but really, I was feeling just as amazed as she, and I was really thinking that things might be different there in Ivitachuco. Perhaps, I thought, Vitachuco is a great enough chief that the Españols will not be able to do to him and his people what they have done elsewhere. Or perhaps the alliance Vitachuco is considering will also be attractive to De Soto. I hoped that I was correct. I was sick of the violence and brutality. I had even begun to think that maybe I was witnessing the first stages of the end of the world.

"As the evening moved on into night, it was easy to maintain my happy illusion that all might be well this time. Vitachuco's people had indeed prepared a tremendous feast. There was all manner of food set before us: venison, opossum, rabbit and squirrel. There were various kinds of fish and other seafood. And there was grain from the storehouses of Ivitachuco. Some of it had been made into bread. There were stews and other good things to eat. I remember thinking that the gardens of Ivitachuco must be vast in order to supply enough to last this late into the year. And the steaming food and the fires here and there around the town took the chill out of the night air.

"Then the people of Ivitachuco danced and sang a variety of dances. They were different, but not so different, from the dances of the Real People. I, myself, have seen much stranger dances and heard stranger songs during my days in the west, among the Fierce People, for example. And, of course, the Españols even have their own songs and dances, and they were truly strange to my eyes and ears.

"Anyway, the festivities continued throughout the evening, and eventually Vitachuco himself made his appearance. He came out of the central townhouse in all his splendor. His entire body, all of it that showed, was covered in tattoos. He wore a finely decorated breechclout and moccasins and an elaborate headdress of multicolored feathers from various of the exotic birds in the country to the south of us. And draped over his shoulders was a mantle made from the skin of a large spotted cat. He carried in his right hand a long and elaborately carved staff, and he was flanked on both sides by close advisors, each of whom was dressed only slightly less splendidly than was he.

"When Vitachuco emerged thus from the townhouse, all noise in the town ceased. A crier then came forward to announce the chief's appearance, and it was the same man who had brought us the message and then guided us on in to the town. After he had made the announcement, he singled me out and approached me.

" 'Vitachuco is ready to meet your chief,' he said. 'Bring him forward.'

"Timidly I approached my master, Capitán Viviano García, and I told him what the man had said. García turned to De Soto and spoke to him.

" 'That is the chief, Vitachuco,' he said, 'over there. He wants to meet you now.'

" 'Then by all means,' I heard the governor say, 'let us oblige the savage king.'

"He laid aside the platter of food from which he had been eating and stood up with a loud belch. Then he expanded his chest and raised his chin, holding his head up high in a haughty manner.

" 'Gallegos,' he said, 'stand on my right hand. García, my left. And bring along your talking slave. I'm sure that we'll need him in order to converse with this tawny monarch.'

" '*Sí*, Excellency,' said García. 'Come along, Juan José.'

"The four of us approached Vitachuco; De Soto, Gallegos and García boldly, I like a mouse.

"Vitachuco calmly looked all of us over for a moment before he said anything. Then he spoke in a low voice to his messenger and crier. That man then turned to me.

" 'Greetings from my chief, the great and powerful Vitachuco,' he said. 'He bids you welcome to his land.'

"I turned to De Soto to translate, but I chose not to translate everything.

" 'The Chief Vitachuco says that you are welcome,' I said.

" 'Tell him that Hernando De Soto, *Adelantado* of Cuba and Governor of all of Florida, accepts his hospitality,' said De Soto. I turned back to my fellow translator.

" 'This is Hernando De Soto,' I said. I could not find ways to translate the governor's titles in the trade language, and besides, I did not want to tell Vitachuco that De Soto thought of himself as governor of all of Florida. That would have included Ivitachuco and could have easily, I thought, precipitated an immediate clash between the two men. 'He is the leader of this group, and he is grateful for your hospitality.'

"My words were again translated to Vitachuco, who again spoke. His words were again translated for me.

" 'Vitachuco,' I said, 'would like to know what brings you to this land.'

" 'Tell him that I search for gold,' said De Soto. Even now as I think back on it, I am constantly amazed at the bluntness of these Españols.

" 'He is searching for the yellow metal,' I said. 'The yellow metal is their wealth.'

"After the same process of translation, I spoke again to the governor.

" 'Vitachuco says that he has no yellow metal. It means nothing to him, and it is not to be found in Ivitachuco. He would, however, like to sit down in council with you and speak of a trade alliance and a pact of friendship.'

" 'He has nothing of interest to me to trade unless he has gold,' said De Soto, 'and if he refuses to tell me where I can find the gold, then he can be no friend to me. I know there is gold here, and I mean to get it. Tell him that. Tell him that if he leads me to gold, we will talk of friendship and trade.'

"Those words were harsh, and I struggled for a way to pass them on to Vitachuco without seeming too offensive, but I fear that it was not possible to do so without being inaccurate. I did the best I could, and even then I spoke the words with my head hanging down. Vitachuco's face grew stern. His response was brief.

" 'There is yellow metal to the north,' he said, 'across the next river. There is none here. We will talk more in the morning.'

"He turned abruptly and walked back into the townhouse, his two advisors following along. The messenger paused briefly, then hurried after them. Gallegos and García each looked at De Soto questioningly. De Soto just stood there for a long and tense moment. He stroked his hairy chin and stared after Vitachuco out of the corners of his eyes, his head slightly cocked to one side.

" 'Excellency,' said Gallegos at last, 'shall we clap him in irons?'

" 'No,' said De Soto. 'It's all right. We'll talk some more in the morning.'

Thirteen

I DID NOT KNOW IT at the time, of course, but the events which took place later that night made it perfectly clear that the clash which I had feared had, in fact, occurred. The two powerful leaders, De Soto and Vitachuco, both men of great pride, had both, even as they stared at each other and spoke to each other through interpreters, developed a strong hatred one for the other, and each had been planning for action.

"We camped outside the town that night. That was the first hint that I had of trouble to come. Everywhere else we had been, the Españols, whether or not De Soto had been present, had simply displaced townspeople from their own homes and moved themselves in.

"I remember wondering why we did not do that there at Ivitachuco. Was it because De Soto was afraid of the strength of Vitachuco and his people? I thought not. The power of Vitachuco was impressive, but De Soto seemed to have no fear.

"It had not been long after Vitachuco's abrupt departure

that De Soto had ordered all of his party out of the town. There was a vast prairie immediately west of the town, and it was there that we went.

" 'Gallegos,' he had said, 'set up our camp at the far edge of this prairie.'

"And Gallegos had led the way and given the orders. The camp had been made and fires lit, and the men were preparing to put themselves to bed for the night. I had just stretched myself out beside a small fire, when I heard De Soto call out again.

" 'Gallegos,' he roared, and I listened hard, for I wanted to know what the governor had in his mind. I was still curious as to why he had taken us out of the town. I was suspicious of his motives. Gallegos answered quickly and ran to the governor's side. Luckily for my curiosity, they were not far from my little fire.

" '*Sí*, Excellency?' said Gallegos.

" 'Gallegos, get the men back into their armor and armed and mounted as quickly as possible,' said De Soto.

" 'At once,' said Gallegos, and he ran to do his master's bidding. Then, of course, I knew what was about to happen, and I was horrified, but there was nothing I could do. I waited, and I think I did not breathe or even blink.

"In a short while, the Españols were mounted up and ready to go. De Soto rode out in front of the ranks to address the men. He turned his mount to face them and fought to hold it still while he spoke.

" 'When I give the command,' he said, 'we will attack. Kill as many as you like, but do not kill the chief. I want him alive. Some of you take brands to fire the village as we go in. This heathen king has insulted me, and that must be avenged.'

"Then he roared a command, and the hoofs of the beasts

thundered against the earth as they charged. I was behind them, breathing their dust. I could see nothing. There were others there with me. Falda was there, of course, and there were Españols who did not have *sogwilis* and were not soldiers. There were also still surviving bearers and other slaves picked up at the towns we had gone through. All of us were left back there at the camp to wait and watch.

"As the deadly attackers raced toward the town, I ran to one side, hoping to get a better view for myself. Falda ran after me, and so did some of the Españols. I don't think that they were running to keep us from escaping. I think they were running for the same reason as I—to get a better view.

"When I at last reached a point where I could see around the attackers to the town, I received my second surprise of the night. Warriors from Vitachuco's town came rushing out to meet the Españols. They could not have responded so quickly to the noise of the attack had they not already been prepared for battle.

"And they had been ready. Vitachuco, like De Soto, had prepared his people for battle as soon as he was able to do so in secret, as soon as De Soto had taken all of his men out of the town. Perhaps if De Soto had waited a little longer before attacking, Vitachuco would have moved first and attacked the camp. I believe that each man had the same idea.

"Then they raced toward each other, wildly waving their weapons. The war cries of the warriors of Ivitachuco sent chills through my body, but they were more than matched by the screams and foul oaths of the crude Españols, the hoofbeats of their *sogwilis* and the clanking of their armor and weapons.

"I felt like I was dreaming, for it seems, even in thinking back, that it took a very long time for the two groups to come together. In reality, it could not have taken very long.

The space they had to travel across the open prairie was not so far across.

"Vitachuco had at least two hundred warriors behind him, and they were brave men and good fighters, but they were outnumbered by the Españols, for there were at least that many mounted men. Then behind the mounted ones came the foot soldiers. And besides that, the armor and the weapons of the Españols were more than the people of Ivitachuco were prepared to deal with. Oh yes, and of course, the big beasts themselves. Still it was not an easy victory for De Soto.

"The chief's warriors scattered at first when the mounted men hit their ranks, but they quickly closed in again to attack the Españols from the rear. As the soldiers tried to turn their beasts, they ran into each other, and some of them fell over. The *Indios* rushed upon the fallen ones and crushed their skulls with warclubs or stabbed them with their knives.

"Some of them jumped up from behind or from the sides to grab the men and pull them off the backs of the beasts. I think that at first the Españols were surprised by the ferocity of this enemy. They had not before met with such resistance. They were used to slaughtering people who did not fight.

"I myself saw Vitachuco in the midst of the battle single-handedly kill three Españols. The chief was wielding only a short flint-bladed knife, but he was as fierce a man in battle as I have ever seen.

"I didn't see who did it, or even notice just when it was started, but soon I realized that the town was in a blaze, and the battlefield then was bathed in an eerie, flickering light. The figures there became for a while either startlingly illuminated or completely shadowed, but after I grew used to the strange light, I could again distinguish one man from another.

"I saw my master hacking at an *Indio* with his long sword. I saw Gallegos in the clutches of another. Both men fell to the ground and rolled over and over in desperate combat. I could not tell just what happened, but in a moment, Gallegos stood up. The other did not. Gallegos was holding in his right hand a short knife, and I thought I could see that its blade was bloody.

"I saw the man who had served as messenger, guide and interpreter to us face a charge from a man still mounted on the back of his *sogwili*. The beast smashed into the man, knocking him to the ground. Then the rider turned the beast and charged again, running the beast over the fallen man, stamping and cutting the man with the sharp hoofs and the great weight.

"I saw much more than that, but the individual moments of the battle have become in my mind a blur of frightful, violent and bloody images. Only one other incident stands out clearly in my memory.

"De Soto had been unseated and was standing on the ground, his sword in hand. Vitachuco must have seen him, for when I looked, the two leaders were standing face-to-face. De Soto swung his sword but missed as the chief jumped back. The battle raged around them, but my attention had become totally fixed upon those two.

"Vitachuco ran at De Soto, ducking low to come in under the long sword. He made an underhand thrust with his knife, but the governor stepped aside and struck the chief on the back as he passed. Vitachuco staggered, but did not fall. He ran on past the governor, stopped and turned. De Soto turned as well, and they faced each other once again.

"Then the governor raised his sword high overhead, holding it with both his hands. He swung it downward as if he meant to slice the chief in half from head to crotch, but once again, Vitachuco stepped aside to avoid the blow. Before De Soto could recover from his swing and raise his sword again, Vitachuco stepped forward and made an upward swipe with his knife that sliced De Soto's face along one side from the lower jawbone to the hairline just above the temple.

"Even from where I watched in the uncertain flickering light, I could tell that it was a severe wound. The blood streamed from it freely.

"De Soto screamed in pain and dropped his sword. He fell to his knees, holding his face in both hands. Blood ran out between the fingers of his left hand and down his arm to his elbow. I felt a thrill race through my body, and I waited for Vitachuco to deliver the death blow.

"But just then, an Español I did not know stepped up behind the chief and ran a long sword into his back and clear through his body. He pulled it out and ran it through again, and then the great chief fell. I turned my face away as I saw the Español raise his sword overhead to hack.

"Soon after that, the battle was over and done. There were a few bodies of Españols, many more of the *Indios*. But many *Indios* had fled, and those who had been in town, the women and children and old men, fled too, I think, when they saw how the fight was going toward the last. The entire town was burned to the ground.

"Back at our camp, I listened for most of the night as De Soto screamed and cursed and moaned while his face wound was tended to by his doctor. I got a glimpse of the wound that night while it was still fresh, and it was a ghastly one. I could see the white of his jawbone at the lower end of the slice. A little farther up, the cheek was cut clear through. If the governor had tried to drink some *ron* that night, the vile liquid would have run out the side of his face. Above the cheek the wound was not so deep, but was at least a bad scratch on up into his hairline.

"He kept me awake that night, but I was glad to hear him suffering. I wished that his pain could be even worse, his injuries more severe. I did not wish him dead, not yet, for there is no suffering, I think, on the other side, and if anyone ever deserved to suffer, it was this bloody Español, this Hernando De Soto, *Adelantado* of Cuba and Governor of all Florida, this monster who was at once both more and less than a man.

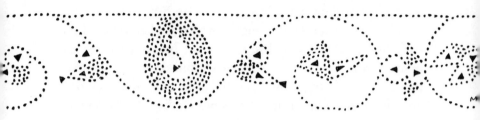

Fourteen

I DID NOT get much sleep that night, and what little I did get was not restful, so when my master kicked me in the buttocks in the morning to wake me up, I had a hard time of it. My eyes did not want to open, and my bones and muscles did not want to lift my weary body. I knew, though, that if I failed to obey, I would get a beating, so I struggled up onto my feet.

"I was amazed to find that we were packing up to move. I had thought that with the governor's severe face wound, we would rest there for a while to give it time to heal. He must have had at least a terrible throbbing pain throughout his face. But, as I said before, the governor was both more and less than a man, and he was mounted up and ready to ride. His head was wrapped in bloody cloth, and the orders were issued out loud by Gallegos, but the governor was ready to ride. For a moment I almost admired him for that.

"But just as I was about to soften a little bit in my feelings toward De Soto, Gallegos roared out an order, and several of the soldiers ran to obey. In another moment, they brought out in front of us hundreds of captives. They had apparently worked throughout the night to round up as many of Vitachuco's surviving warriors as they could find.

"They slaughtered them there in front of us while we watched. Hundreds of them. The grisly process took all of the morning. Only then did we start to march.

"As I trudged along beside the beast of my master for the next two days, I took great though secret pleasure in knowing that De Soto was in pain. I even wished that the pain could have been worse. Still we moved ahead. After two more days we came to another village. Like many others we had seen, it was abandoned. We spent the night there, and in the morning we moved on.

"The next day we came to a slightly larger town, and this time the people were all there at home. They called their town Iviahica, and they were an Apalachee people, I think. They greeted us meekly, and I discovered that they had been among the towns that had paid tribute to Vitachuco. Knowing that De Soto had killed their master, they gave their obeisance to him.

"Perhaps because of De Soto's pain, the meeting there at Iviahica was subdued. They quietly let us in, and we entered quietly. The Españols did, however, follow their old pattern from there on. They displaced people to take over houses for themselves. De Soto's orders, if they were his, and I imagine that they were, were still given voice by Gallegos.

"This was early in *duninuhdi*, the harvest moon, called *Octubre* by the Españols, and now the chill in the air was lasting all day long. We knew that winter would be settling in on us soon, and I wondered just how long De Soto was going to keep us lingering in Iviahica.

"Then I heard that the rest were coming to this place to join us. That meant not only the herdsmen and all of their *sikwas* would be coming, but also the ones that we had left at what I had thought was to be the main camp, the place there where we had landed and where the big boats, I thought, waited for our return, the place that De Soto had named Espíritu Santo.

"Soon, it seemed, there would be crowded into and around the town of Iviahica about six hundred soldiers and another one hundred or so herdsmen, servants and slaves. That was not counting the so-called bearers that the Españols picked up along the way. In addition there were at least two hundred *sogwilis* and, I think, four hundred *sikwas*. There were also animals called *mulas*, which were like the *sogwilis* but smaller and of no gender. In my opinion they were also tougher than the larger beasts. There were also the *yansa*-like oxen and, of course, the large vicious dogs.

"As time went on it became obvious to me that the people of Iviahica were going to be required to support this large and incredible gathering throughout the winter. I knew, of course, that the storehouses of the town would be sorely taxed. In fact I have never yet seen a town that could have managed such an undertaking. Perhaps, I thought, this was the time for De Soto to make use of the *sikwas*. Perhaps he had anticipated the winter and brought the animals along for just that purpose.

"Still we did not kill and eat the *puercos*. But then, the stores of Iviahica were not yet exhausted. I thought that the governor must be waiting for just that moment to make use of his large and unwieldy herd. When we had run out of everything else, I decided, he will have the *sikwas* slaughtered.

"*Nuhdadewi*, the big trading moon, called *Noviembre* by the Españols, arrived. The supplies of grain in the storehouses were getting low enough to cause worry. The hunters of Iviahica were kept busy, going out again almost as soon as they returned. People gathered fish from their traps every day, and traders were sent out to surrounding towns and villages to barter for more grain.

"By the arrival of *uhsgiyi*, the snow moon, *Diciembre* to the *Cristianos,* the storehouses were empty. The corn, beans, squash and other crop foods which we ate, we and the animals, were all obtained by trade, and it was said that even the people with whom we were trading were running dangerously low. The game was depleted for miles around Iviahica, and the streams and rivers seemed to be empty of fish. The hunters wandered farther and farther from home, and the range of the traders was also extended.

"Then *yansa* appeared. I did not see them, but I saw the runner when he came into town shouting the news. Several hunters prepared to go after them, and some of the Españols, including my master García. They rode out and were gone for the rest of that day.

"Late in the evening, they returned. Their *mulas* were loaded with meat and hides, and everyone ate better for a time after that, for they went out again the next day and the next, and each time they were successful. Then the herd of *yansa* was gone and so was the meat it provided.

"When the hunters came back to town after that first day, my master told a story about one of the Españols, a particularly bad-tempered little man named Tiburcio Carrasco.

" 'Carrasco,' my master said, 'like the rest of us, was astonished when he first saw the beasts. Great hairy cattle, they were. I've never seen anything like them. We watched the savages at first. They sneaked up on the beasts on their hands and knees and fired their arrows into them. Some used their crude lances. Carrasco watched with a sneer on his evil little face.'

"The listening Españols laughed at this, and Carrasco spat an oath at my master, and my master laughed at it and continued.

" ' "I can do better than that," little Carrasco said. "Watch me."

" 'He leveled his lance and spurred his mount, and they raced at the herd of big beasts. When he had gone about halfway, the beasts took flight, and Carrasco raced after them. He caught up with the slowest, and as he came up beside it, he nicked its shoulder with his lance. The hairy beast bellowed, stopped, turned and charged. It ran its head into the side of Carrasco's *caballo*, knocking it over on its side, and Carrasco went rolling in the dirt. One of the *Indios* showed up about then and killed the beast with an arrow. I think if he had not done so, Carrasco would have been trampled by the brute.'

"Again the listeners laughed, and again Carrasco grumbled and cursed. Falda was sitting beside me. She leaned close to my ear and whispered, 'I wish that the white man had been trampled.' The Españols did kill some of the animals themselves after that, but Carrasco never lived down the story of his first attempt.

"In the Españols' month of *Enero*, the one we call *Unoluhdani*, or Cold, we were almost desperate, and I thought that surely De Soto would at last allow some of his precious fat *sikwas* to be slaughtered. But he did not. One day I overheard Carrasco, the same man who had tried to kill *yansa* from the back of his *sogwili*, talking with another soldier. They were huddled close together, mumbling and grumbling their complaints.

" 'What the hell did he bring them along for anyway?' Carrasco asked.

" 'They're his God-damned pets,' said the other. 'That's what they are. His *favoritos.*'

" 'Maybe his *amantes?*' said Carrasco, and then they both laughed, for that word implied that perhaps the governor used the animals for women.

" 'Yes, I think so. That's why he won't let us kill them and eat them. He can't remember which one he last diddled.'

" 'Even so,' said Carrasco, growing once again serious, or at least almost so, 'he has four hundred of them. What difference would a few make? We could eat two hundred of them, and he would still have two hundred left to hump. He can only do one at a time.'

"And I must admit that I, too, wondered what difference a few would make and why the governor had brought along so many of these animals that were so much trouble if he was not going to allow them to be eaten. I did not believe that he was using them as Carrasco had suggested, but I did think that the man must be crazy. Still today I think that. The only thing that I really do not understand is why it is that the white men allow those among them who are the most crazy to become their leaders.

"It occurs to me that I may be giving a somewhat false impression of life in Iviahica during the long winter of De Soto's stay there. I have been talking only about the tremendous demand for food that resulted from that stay, and that did, of course, place a heavy burden on the shoulders of the unhappy residents of that town. But other things were going on as well, things that I had unfortunately grown used to since falling into the hands of Capitán Viviano García.

"Many people had been displaced in order that the Españols have comfortable quarters for themselves. That meant that the people who were forced out of their own homes had to be crowded into the homes of others. All of the people were affected by this movement.

"And as always, De Soto made demands of the people. He demanded that they feed him and his army and animals. He demanded that the hunters hunt and the traders trade and the fishermen fish. His demands were met because he kept the chief of the town hostage, and the people knew that if they failed to meet his demands, their chief would be executed.

"The Españols took young women for their own uses. They took young unmarried women, and they took women away from their husbands. There were also among them a few who preferred young men, and they, too, had their way.

"On several occasions Españols beat people for little or no reason. These hairy men have terrible tempers, and they seem to enjoy inflicting pain and injury on others. The stay at Iviahica was the longest period of inactivity they had endured on their expedition, so now and then they engaged in violence, it seemed to me, just for the fun of it.

"It was in *Kakali*, Bony, the moon called *Febrero* by the white men, that the sickness struck. People began to cough, a little at first. Then they coughed more. Some coughed up blood. And they grew weak from the sickness. And the sickness spared no one. Old people and very small children and everyone in between were struck by it. Some of the Españols were sick, but they did not suffer from it the way that the *Indios* suffered. And no Español died from it. But the *Indios* died. Many died.

"Their doctor tried to cure them, but he was completely frustrated. He had never seen anything like this sickness before, and therefore he had no method of treating it. He tried different things. He sang songs. He prepared medicines, some to drink, some to eat, some to rub on the victims' skins.

He put the victims in sweat baths, and he took them to the water. He killed buzzards and hung the bodies on the fronts of the houses, but even that did no good. Nothing worked. The people died. Many of them died. There was much mourning and wailing and singing of death songs.

"And it was a time of heavy rains then, too, as it often is in *Kakali*. The winds came from the south, bringing with them cold rain. I heard my master García say one day that the dampness would only make the sickness worse. He did not say what the sickness was, but since he seemed to know about it, and the doctor at Iviahica did not, I thought that the sickness must have been something that the Españols brought with them, another way for them to kill *Indios*. Perhaps, but I don't know.

"Not all died from the strange sickness, of course. Some of us were spared. I don't know why.

"In *anuhyi*, the windy moon, the Españols' *Marzo*, we packed up to leave Iviahica. The wound on the governor's face was healed, but it had left a terrible scar on his face that made him appear even more fearful and ugly than before. Many of the residents of Iviahica were still sick, among them their chief. Many had already died.

"As we left that town, I remember thinking that for once we were leaving without having first slaughtered large numbers of people. One of the reasons the governor had not killed the people was that they had told him about another place, and he had believed them. So we were leaving without having set fire to the people's homes and without having killed them, but we left them sick and dying and almost without food. Perhaps the people of Iviahica suffered more than all the others after all.

"So we left Iviahica, a place that had been our home for so long a time, a place which we left utterly changed from what it had been. We headed north. We were looking for a place called Anhayca Apalachee, a land of yellow metal governed by a woman, for that is what the chief of Iviahica had told De Soto.

"We took with us enough provisions for sixty days, leaving the mostly sick people of Iviahica with nothing for themselves. But almost all of the slaves had died during the winter of cold and lack of food and the sickness. So the Españols for once carried their own burdens. I thought that it was a small price for them to pay for all of the death and destruction they had caused. They were far from done. They would cause much more yet.

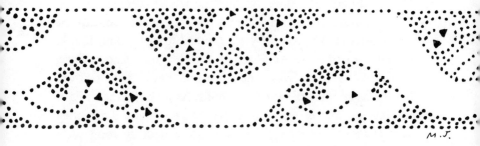

Fifteen

WE LEFT IVIAHICA early in the windy moon, and I for one was glad to be moving again. It is a very uncomfortable feeling to sit idly by and watch while people are constantly being oppressed, and the oppression of the Españols is particularly brutal. I think that I had almost given up on the idea of ever being free of these *Cristianos*. I thought that I would die their slave. I was already feeling like an old man.

"We marched north, searching for this place of yellow metal. The Españols called it a golden kingdom, ruled over by a *reina*, a queen. I was not sure what was meant by that word at first, but eventually I learned. They have in their own country one man or one woman who is ruler over all and has the power of life and death over all of their people, who are called their subjects.

"The Españols grumbled much because they were forced to act as their own bearers, their former captives almost all having died over the winter. And De Soto did not acquire any additional bearers from Iviahica. Practically everyone there had been very sick by the time we left them.

"At the end of our first day on the trail again, we camped beside a river. The next day we crossed it with no difficulty, but later in the day we reached a wider and deeper river. The crossing there was much more difficult. De Soto ordered a large raft or barge to be built. As with the building of bridges, large trees were cut down and trimmed. Then they were lashed together tightly to create a wide floating platform which would accommodate many men and animals at one time. Even so, it took many crossings back and forth to move everyone to the other side. The whole process took four days to complete.

"After one more day's travel we came to a village. It was on a peninsula that jutted out into a swampy river, and it was called by the residents there Capachequi. At this place, De Soto acquired some more bearers, and the Españols were much relieved. He did it in the usual way, by threatening the life of the town chief. We rested there for a few days, then went on to a place which the Españols called White Springs.

"There was no village there, but it was a good place to camp, and the spring was full of fish. We caught many fish and ate well. We stayed only one night, leaving early the next morning. In the middle of the next day we arrived at a wide river. The water was fast and rough, and so De Soto ordered a bridge to be built.

"The Españols constructed their bridge in the same manner as they had before, but the bridge collapsed, and the logs were carried away in the swift waters. I thought that perhaps Long Man, the spirit of the river, had seen enough of these intruders and had decided to take action against them.

"They cut more trees and built another bridge, and then they started to cross. Four mounted Españols went onto the bridge, and when the leader was about halfway across, the bridge suddenly leaned to one side. We could hear the timbers creaking. The men on the bridge shouted, and the *sogwilis* screamed hideously. Then it fell over, carrying the four men and the four animals with it down into the water. There was much shouting and running back and forth.

"Some of the men on land threw lines out into the water, trying in vain to reach their companions. Two of the men in the water clung to their *sogwilis*, and the animals managed to swim to dry land. The other two men swam alone and made it safely to the shore. A third *sogwili* swam to safety, but the fourth was lost, swept away and drowned.

"Then an Español named Tobar sat down with De Soto and Gallegos. My master García was there too. Tobar drew some pictures in the dirt and talked to them about the way bridges were built. I did not understand what he was saying, but he was telling them another way to build, I think. At last De Soto stood up.

" 'Do it,' he said. 'You're in charge.'

"Gallegos did not appear to be happy with this new arrangement, but he had no choice. The governor had spoken. This Tobar was in charge of the construction. Again they cut down trees and trimmed them, and again they lashed them together in a way to span the river.

"I know nothing of building bridges, so I cannot tell you what Tobar did differently from what had been done before. I did think that I could see how the logs which supported the bridge were set at different angles here and there from what the previous ones had been.

"At any rate, Tobar's bridge held up, and the crossing was completed. Four days later we reached a pine wood near another river. This time we did not cross. We turned east and followed the river for another day, and we came to a large village there. It was called Toa.

"We stayed there one night, and the next day De Soto ordered more bearers to be taken. He also took more food from the village. Then we started to travel again. The governor seemed to be in much more of a hurry at this point than he had been before, for we started to travel again as soon as he had taken what he wanted. It was the middle of the day.

"He was in such a rush that he took with him only forty men, leaving Tobar in charge of the rest with orders to hurry along behind as best they could. Gallegos went with De Soto, as did my master García. My master took me and Falda along, and De Soto had no objections to that, as he thought that we might be needed as interpreters.

"We traveled the rest of that day and well into the darkness before the governor allowed us to stop and rest for the night. Then we started out again early the next morning, and did not stop at all after dark. It must have been about the middle of the night when we arrived at the river. It was not deep, but it was fast, and the crossing was treacherous. Gallegos suggested that we camp and cross in the morning when we could see better, but De Soto disagreed.

" 'We move on,' he ordered. 'Start the crossing.'

"He, himself, led the way, kicking his big *sogwili* in the sides and rushing headlong into the cold and fast-moving water. Gallegos roared out an order for the rest to follow, and he too raced forward. My master followed soon after, and I and Falda ran into the water, trying to keep abreast of his big *sogwili*.

"It was terrible confusion, running along in the cold water on the hidden rocks with uncertain footing, hoping that the *sogwilis* would not lurch to the side and knock us over, the snorts and wheezings of the animals, the splashing sounds, the clanking of armor and weapons and the shouts and curses of the Españols all ringing in our ears. And all of this in near blackness.

"Falda clutched my arm tightly as we struggled to keep up and to get across. I'm not sure how far along we were when it happened, but I slipped and fell, dragging her down with me. I fell clear under the cold water, and she landed on top of me. We struggled to rise again, and I swallowed some water. I came up coughing, pulling Falda along after me, and just as we were about to regain our footing, an Español on a *sogwili* passed by us very close. We were so startled that we almost fell down again.

"At last we made it across. It could not have really taken all that long, but it seemed to take forever. We were again on solid, dry land, but we were soaked to our bones, and the night was chilly. I tried to hold Falda close to me as we walked, for my own teeth were chattering, and I knew that she too was cold.

"Somehow we made it through the rest of that incredibly long night, and when the Sun came out from under the eastern edge of the Sky Vault and climbed up a ways along its underside, the day grew warmer, and eventually our clothes dried, and our bodies warmed up again. But Falda was sneezing and sniffling, and I was afraid for her, remembering the sickness back at Iviahica.

"We traveled for another day, rested a night, and on the next day we came to another broad river. I hated to get myself wet again, and I was particularly worried about Falda, but at least we would not be crossing in the darkness. On the way across this river, an Español fell from the back of his *sogwili*. He screamed for help as he was swept along in the cold waters. Some of the men tried to rescue him, but he was gone so quickly that their efforts were all in vain.

"My feelings wrestled with each other after that. It was a horrible thing to watch a man carried away by the waters of Long Man while his friends were helpless. But it was an Español, a cruel man who had killed many himself, and once again, it occurred to me that Long Man was taking revenge against these intruders for what they were doing to his people.

"We moved on. The governor seemed not much concerned, but his men were quiet, almost somber, following the loss of their comrade. It surprised me a little to find that they really did, after all, have human emotions, but there may have been another explanation. Perhaps they thought, If the governor is so little concerned with the loss of that man, will he care at all when my turn comes? Perhaps that thought was the source of their strange and quiet mood.

"We had not gone far from the site of the drowning when we were met by some *Indios*. They looked as if they were waiting for our arrival, and De Soto called my master to him when he spotted the men. I was not far behind, so I could hear their conversation.

" 'García,' said the scar-faced governor, 'bring your talking slave forward.'

" 'Juan José,' shouted my master, 'come forward to me.'

"I moved up to join García and De Soto, keeping Falda close beside me. She had begun to cough, and I did not want to lose sight of her if I could help it.

" '*Sí, Capitán?*' I said.

" 'Stand by,' he said, and he turned back toward De Soto. 'What are your orders, Excellency?' he asked.

" 'Take that savage with you and approach those men,' said the governor. 'Find out where they come from and what they're doing here. Ask them where to find the golden kingdom.'

"We walked forward to meet with the men who waited there, my master and I and Falda. When we were close enough for conversation, they spoke first.

" 'Hello,' said the man standing in the middle. He used the trade language. 'We were sent here to meet you. We are from the town of Ichisi.'

"I greeted them in return and explained to them that I had to translate for my master the Español. Then I told García what they had said.

" 'Why have they been sent to meet us and by whom?' he asked, and I turned and asked the question of the messengers.

" 'Our chief, Camumo, sent us. He told us to guide you to Ichisi where you will be our honored guests.'

"I did not know what the motive of this Camumo might be. Several possibilities occurred to me: that he might be afraid of De Soto because he had heard of what had happened behind us, and he might be thinking that if he offered friendship, aid and assistance before it was demanded, things would go better for him and his people. Or that he might be looking for powerful allies against his enemies. A third possibility that came to mind was that Camumo might be attempting to lead the Españols into a trap. I told García what the messenger had said.

" 'Ask him about the land of gold,' said my master. I turned back toward the messengers.

" 'The leader of these people is looking for a land of the yellow metal,' I said. 'He was told that it is ruled over by a woman chief. Do you know of such a place?'

"The three messengers looked at me for a moment, then looked at one another and conversed in their own tongue, which I could not understand. Then the spokesman turned back toward me.

" 'We do not know of such a place, but perhaps Camumo knows something about it. He's much wiser than we are. Will you follow us to Ichisi?'

"Again I translated their words for my master.

" 'Stay here,' he said to me, and he wheeled his mount around and rode back to De Soto. I watched him for a moment, then whispered to Falda.

" 'Should I try to warn these people, do you think?'

" 'You can try,' she said, 'but I do not think that they will listen to you.'

"I looked at the spokesman in the group of messengers. He was a proud-looking man, young and strong, and he had tattoos on his body which I took to mean that he had won honors in battle.

" 'What do you know of these men?' I asked him.

" 'We have heard many things,' he said, and I could tell that he was suspicious of me for asking that question.

" 'Have you heard what has happened to the people behind us? The ones whose villages we have visited?'

" 'We have heard that some were destroyed,' he said, 'and we have heard that some were not.'

" 'Those that were destroyed suffered that fate because they did not deliver what our leader demanded of them,' I said. 'He looks for the yellow metal. If you cannot provide it, he will kill you.'

" 'We have nothing to fear,' said the messenger. 'We have come in friendship to lead your masters to our village and treat them as guests. We will help them all we can. That's what Camumo has said.'

" 'You had better be careful what you say,' said another of the messengers to me. 'If your masters hear you talking of them in this way, they might kill you.'

" 'The Españols cannot understand a word of what we're

saying,' I replied, and I'm afraid that I said the words with just a touch of smugness in my voice. About then I heard the sounds of the *sogwilis*' hoofs, and I turned to see De Soto and the rest riding toward us. As De Soto came closer, he yelled out to me.

" 'Tell them to lead on,' he said. 'Lead us on to their town.'

Sixteen

THE MESSENGERS from Ichisi led us north, and we traveled for four days. De Soto and his Españols began to grow suspicious of their intentions. De Soto called my master to his side and spoke to him in a low voice, and my master then rode back to where Falda and I walked along beside the mounted column.

" 'Juan José,' said García, 'talk to those men again. Ask them where is this Ichisi. We've been traveling four days now, and the governor thinks that we should have arrived there already.'

"I ran forward to where the messengers walked in front of us and stepped alongside of the one who was their spokesman.

" 'My masters want to know how much farther to your town,' I said.

" 'Just ahead is a great river,' he answered. 'Once we have crossed the river, Ichisi is not far. Less than a day's walk from the river.'

"I reported back to my master, and he to De Soto, and we

continued to follow the messengers from Ichisi. It wasn't long before we came to the river. There were canoes waiting for us there at the water's edge. They belonged to these men from Ichisi.

" 'Here we cross the water,' said the messenger. I repeated his words to my master. De Soto heard my words. He looked at the river and then at the canoes. He shrugged and dismounted.

" 'Come along, Gallegos,' he said. 'García, appoint some men to swim the *caballos* across.'

"The Españols, all but the ones named by my master, rode across in the canoes. It took the messengers several trips back and forth to take them all. The men appointed by my master to swim the *sogwilis* across the river were actually done with their chore before the last of the canoes had made its crossing. That done, we continued north. It was still daylight when we reached Ichisi.

"The chief of Ichisi came out to greet us, and I could tell, at least I thought that I could, that the chief was surprised and perhaps a little frightened at the strength of the army of *Cristianos*. I imagine that he was at once reevaluating his former plans, whatever they might have been.

"The chief was standing in front of his house, flanked by his advisors, and the governor rode right up to him without dismounting. He sat in his saddle and looked down on the chief. Immediately behind De Soto were the other thirty-nine mounted and heavily armed Españols. I was called to the front to stand beside the governor's *sogwili*.

" 'Tell him that I am Hernando De Soto,' said the governor, *'Adelantado* of all of Cuba and Governor of Florida, and tell him that I am a child of the Sun. Tell him that, talking slave.'

"I stepped toward the chief just a little.

" 'I am speaking for these Españols,' I said, 'for these white men. Do you understand the trade language?'

" 'Yes, I do,' said the chief. 'Tell the white men that I welcome them in peace.'

" 'I will, of course,' I said, 'but first, I have been made to tell you that this man here before you is called Hernando De Soto. He is the ruler of all of this land, and he is the child of the Sun. That is what he told me to say.'

"Then I turned back to the governor, but I kept my head down and looked at the ground while I spoke.

" 'I have told him what you said,' I said to De Soto, 'and he told me to bid you welcome.'

" 'Tell him that we are all hungry and would eat,' said the governor.

"The rest of that day was taken up in feeding the Españols and their animals, and the people of Ichisi fed us very well indeed. When the governor was satisfied, he called me to him again to pass along his next order. It was to have the people vacate enough houses to accommodate us for the night. That was done quickly, and we moved into the houses of the displaced persons to spend the night. Some of the Españols selected women from Ichisi to spend the night with. No objections were voiced by the chief or the people of Ichisi. It was not that they had no objections. They were afraid.

"The following morning De Soto had the chief and all of the people brought out into the town square. He informed the chief, through me, that he needed bearers and corn grinders, and he selected about twenty men and women from among the youngest and healthiest there. The horrified chief watched as the irons were placed around the necks of his people and the chain was attached, linking them all together.

"I thought that we were ready to leave after the governor had chained the new slaves, but we did not leave just then. We stayed the rest of that day. The next day, De Soto demanded a meeting with the chief.

" 'I am looking for the richest province and the greatest ruler in these parts,' he said. 'Tell that to the chief.'

" 'Our leader is looking for the most powerful chief around here,' I said in the trade language, 'and he is looking for the yellow metal. Can you tell him where to find those things?'

"The chief looked hesitant, so I quickly spoke again.

" 'If you do not tell him something that he wants to hear, he may kill you or some of your people,' I said.

" 'He wants to go to Ocute,' said the chief. 'Ocute is the place he is looking for.'

"I wondered if there was such a place as Ocute, and if there was, if it was inhabited by enemies of this chief. I told the governor what the chief had said.

" 'Is this Ocute ruled by a woman?' asked the governor. I repeated his question to the chief.

" 'No,' he said. 'It is not. It has a powerful chief who is called by the same name as his town: Ocute.'

"De Soto frowned at this news and stared for a long moment at the chief.

" 'Tell him that I was told by someone else that the kingdom of gold was ruled by a *reina*,' he said. 'I want to know who is lying to me.'

"I told the chief more or less what the governor had said, and the chief surprised me with a quick response.

" 'I've heard of that place,' he said, 'but I've never been there. It's farther away from here than is Ocute, but Ocute is on the way to that place.'

"De Soto wanted to know the name of the place that was ruled by a woman. I asked the chief.

" 'Cofitachequi,' he said.

" 'Then,' said the governor, 'we will go to Ocute on the way to Cofitachequi. Tell this chief to provide me with a guide.'

"The guide was provided, yet still we did not leave the town. We spent another night there. The next day some of the Españols set up a cross on the central mound of Ichisi. I was bold enough to ask my master García what the cross was for.

" 'It's the sign of our savior,' he said. 'It means that Christ rules over this land.'

" 'I thought that the governor ruled over this land,' I said.

" 'Yes, of course, Juan José,' said García, 'but the governor rules through Christ.'

"I did not understand him then, and I still do not know what García meant by that. I do not know who this Christ is either. I never saw the man. And I have no idea why, after going through so many towns and villages, staying in many of them, destroying some, the governor chose Ichisi as the first town in which to set up his sign of Christ.

"The next day we left Ichisi, the guide leading us north, the new bearers carrying the burdens. *Kawoni*, the flower moon, had arrived. The Españols called it *Abril*. We slept that night in open country and started out early again the next morning. We traveled that day through a populous river valley, but that population was fortunate that the governor was in a hurry to find Ocute and Cofitachequi. They were hardly molested as we passed through.

"The next day we did stop at a village, where the governor again demanded some more bearers and some more food, and while we were there, the chief of Ocute himself arrived to meet us. He was accompanied by several warriors. In spite of the fact that Ocute had come voluntarily to meet the governor, had caused many presents to be sent and had volunteered to guide us the rest of the way to his town, De Soto had him taken prisoner. Even after all I had seen, I thought this an outrage.

"We spent the night there in some houses after kicking out the people who lived in them. The next day, our hostage led us on into his town. There was no yellow metal to be found, and the governor had Ocute himself, as well as the guide who had led us from Ichisi, killed before the entire population of the town.

" 'I will not be lied to by ignorant savages,' he said.

"We stayed in Ocute for three days, and on the third day, the rest of De Soto's men arrived, including those who drove the unruly herd of *sikwas*. Once again, the entire contingent was together. When we left Ocute, I thought that we were like a flock of locusts leaving behind us bare fields.

"We traveled for three days and came to another town. The chief there was named Tatofa. His people spoke a language that sounded to me like the language of our *Ani-Chahta* neighbors. I felt a secret thrill run through my body, for I knew that I must be nearing my own home after so many years away. Once again, I dared to entertain thoughts of escape. But I also feared for my people.

"We stayed overnight in Tatofa's town. The next morning the governor took several hundred people as bearers. With all of his people and animals back together, his need for slaves was greater again. Tatofa provided guides and told the governor that Cofitachequi was nine or ten days' march away. The governor's eyes seemed to light up like small campfires at night.

"We traveled north. The next night we spent by a small

stream. Another day we traveled without coming across any villages. We did have to cross a very wide river, but it was not so deep. We camped that night in a forest. The next day was much the same, as was the next night. We traveled another day, crossed another river and spent yet another night beside another small stream.

"When we awoke the next morning, De Soto did not order us to pack and start out immediately. He called Gallegos to his side. I was not far away, sitting with Falda and my master awaiting orders. Falda was coughing, a dry, worrisome cough.

" 'We should have found the place by now,' I overheard De Soto say. 'Bring those heathen guides to me at once.'

"But the guides were nowhere to be found, and De Soto flew into a rage when informed of the fact.

" 'How could they have escaped? Who is guilty of neglect here? I want to know. Gallegos, find the men who are responsible for allowing those guides to escape and bring them to me.'

"I don't believe that anyone was ever found on whom to place the blame, and after raving wildly for a while, the governor decided that we should move on. Without guides, we continued north, and toward the end of the day, we came to a very large river which divided itself into two branches. No one among us had any idea which direction to go. We had no guides. We knew of no villages nearby.

" 'Governor,' I heard Gallegos say, 'we are lost. Hopelessly lost in this wilderness.'

" 'Never hopelessly,' said De Soto. 'Send scouts in all directions to see what they can find.'

"Four Españols rode east and four rode west along the riverbank. Four others were sent southwest, and four southeast. He did not send anyone north. I don't know why. Perhaps he did not want to cross the wide river, or maybe he was afraid to go farther north without guides. The scouts had orders to return before dark. At the end of the day they had all returned, and none of them had anything to report.

" 'We are hopelessly lost,' I heard Gallegos say. But this time he said it to someone other than the governor, and he said it in a whispered voice.

"Our food supply was very low. No one ate much that day. The next day we ate even less. The scouts were sent out again, and again they returned before dark without any encouraging news.

"The third day, the scouts rode out, and we all stayed very hungry all day. The fourth day we had nothing to eat. The scouts found nothing. I was worried more and more about Falda. She was sick, and she needed food to get well.

" 'The men are starving, Governor,' I heard Gallegos say.

" 'Surely we'll find something soon,' said the governor. 'Tell the men to hold up and be brave.'

"On the fifth day, the governor at long last relented. Even under the difficult circumstances we were in, it was hard to believe that the scar-face actually allowed some of his precious *sikwas* to be slaughtered for food.

" 'A pound of pork per man,' he said. 'No more.'

"There were three hundred of the squealing animals at least, and I thought for a moment that the angry soldiers would rebel against their own leader, but they did not. They set about killing the wretched things and carving them into morsels. The meat was carefully weighed with a device the *Cristianos* have for doing that, and each man was given a precise small amount. They called it a pound.

"Later in the day when everyone was again very hungry, the soldiers began calling for more pork. The governor resisted for a while. Then he gave in. But just as the men were about to begin slaughtering again, one of the groups of scouts led by a man named Juan Anasco came riding back.

" 'Governor,' he called out as he raced his *sogwili* in among us. 'Governor, I have found a village.'

" 'Gallegos,' shouted the governor. 'Stop the slaughter at once.'

Seventeen

DE SOTO turned immediately to Gallegos. His eyes were flashing with excitement, and the scar on the side of his face seemed to glow red.

" 'Get everyone mounted,' he said. 'We'll follow Anasco to this village.'

"The governor hurried to his own *sogwili* and climbed onto its back. Then he rode to the side of Anasco. 'Lead on,' he shouted.

"Behind him, Gallegos called out to the rest, 'Get mounted. The rest of you, pack everything up as quickly as you can and follow along. There is food and shelter ahead.'

"I gave my master a questioning look as he mounted his *sogwili* to ride after the others. They were moving fast, and I was afraid that I and Falda would not be able to keep up.

" 'Travel with the bearers and foot soldiers,' he said, and he rode away, leaving me in his dust. I put an arm around Falda as she looked up at me for just an instant. I thought that I could see in her face that she was depending on me to protect her, and that thought frightened me more than a little bit. I was in no position to protect her. I couldn't even protect myself. I was feeling older and more worn out all the time.

"At that very moment, in fact, I was afraid, for my master had ridden ahead with De Soto and Gallegos and the others. I was left, therefore, to the mercy of the foot soldiers, who already felt that García was too easy on me.

"With all of the mounted soldiers gone, a man named Vásquez was left in charge. The riders were not even out of sight when he began shouting orders at everyone.

" 'Pack up everything and load it up,' he said. 'Load up those *mulas* and those slaves. What's left over, put on your own backs. Hurry it up. Get moving. You swineherds, get our governor's herd of pet pigs moving. There's a town ahead. Food, shelter and fresh women. Let's go.'

"My master García had left most of his belongings behind for me to bring along, so I quickly busied myself with packing. Otherwise, Vásquez would have been at me in an instant. Falda helped me, but she was coughing worse than ever. I wanted to tell her to rest and leave the work to me, but I dared not, not under the evil eyes of Vásquez.

"It did not take very long for us to be packed and moving, but it was long enough that the mounted men were well beyond our vision. It was not difficult, though, to follow their trail. We trudged along after them. The trail dust made Falda's coughing grow worse.

"We walked for most of the rest of that day, and I remember being afraid that it would grow dark before we could reach our destination. There was even a moment when I wondered if there really was a town ahead, but I soon told myself that was a foolish thought. There was no reason for Anasco to announce a town if there had been none. Then I saw the smoke ahead from the village fires.

"We were there before dark after all, and I found my master as quickly as I could. I wanted his protection. I had been lucky on the trail without him. I suppose that Vásquez and the others had been in too big a hurry to reach the village to bother with me. The swineherds, as they were called, and their noisy charges were still some distance behind.

"While searching for my master, I had noticed that there did not seem to be many people in the village. I saw four men, *Indios*, standing dejected before De Soto, and I saw no evidence of any other residents.

" 'Master,' I said, 'we're here.'

" 'Good,' said García. 'You're wanted. Come along with me.'

" 'But master,' I said, 'Falda is ill. I'm worried about her.'

" 'Later, Juan José,' said García. 'Come on now.'

"I had no choice. I followed my master. He led me to where De Soto stood staring at the four men. As García was leading me up there to him, the governor saw me coming.

" 'Ah,' he said. 'Good. Good. It's about time the fools arrived. This town was abandoned before we could get here, talking slave, but we found these four. See if you can talk to them.'

"I approached the four men slowly. They saw me, but they looked at the ground.

" 'Do you speak the trade language?' I asked them, speaking to them in that jargon.

"Two of them simply continued to stare at the ground in front of their feet. One gave a slow nod of his head. The fourth one spoke out, almost boldly.

" 'Yes,' he said. 'I do.'

"I turned back toward De Soto.

" 'Governor,' I said, 'I can speak with them. At least with this one. He speaks the trade language, as I do.'

" 'Ask him the way to Cofitachequi,' demanded the governor. I turned back to the captive and asked the governor's question.

" 'I don't know such a place,' said the man.

" 'Are you certain? It's said to be a land of the yellow metal with a woman as its chief. It's dangerous for you to give no answer to this man here.'

" 'I don't know this place you speak of. I don't believe there is any such place.'

"I turned back to De Soto and gave him the man's answer, and as I did, I braced myself for one of the governor's bursts of anger. He surprised, almost startled me by remaining calm. He turned and casually looked over the village around him. Not far away was the townhouse, and in front of it, the square. At one edge of the square a pole was standing. De Soto stared in that direction for a long and silent moment.

" 'Gallegos,' he said at last, his voice still calm, 'take that man and bind him fast to that pole over there.'

" '*Sí*, Excellency,' said Gallegos. He motioned to two other men to follow him, and they took the man by his arms and made him walk over to the pole. They pulled his arms behind his back and tied his wrists behind the pole.

" 'Bind his feet as well,' said the governor, and so they did. 'Now, Gallegos, have some men gather wood and pile it at his feet. A great pile of wood. Pile it all around the pole.'

"In another few moments that too had been done, and I felt the too familiar horror rising up again within me. How much longer? I asked myself. How much more of this will I suffer? I thought that perhaps I should fling myself at the governor and at least die in the act of attacking my enemy, but something else in me said that would be a useless way to die. It would save no one. Of course, I was saving no one anyway, no one but myself.

"Then at a nod from De Soto the pile of wood was set on fire. The man tied to the pole showed no fear, only defiance. He did not yell or scream as the flames began to lick at his flesh. He began to sweat, and when the pain became worse and worse, he winced, but he did not scream. It was only after we could all smell his flesh cooking that the intense pain mercifully caused him to lose consciousness. Then, of course, he was burned to death. The Españols watched the whole thing as if it had been a casual and amusing entertainment. Some smiled. A few actually chuckled out loud. I myself was feeling faint. My head swam.

" 'Juan José,' I heard my master call sharply. 'Can't you hear?'

"I had not heard anything before that, but apparently De Soto had called for me, and I, of course, had failed to answer. I tried to shake myself out of my fog and fight off the faint that I still felt was coming upon me.

" 'Yes, master?' I said.

" 'The governor has called for you, fool. Attend to him here at once.'

"I ran back over to the governor, my head down as if in shame.

" '*Sí*, Excellency?' I said. 'I am here at your service.'

" 'Talk to these three again, talking slave. See if they have answers for me now. Tell them if they do not, they will each suffer a like fate. One at a time.'

"Slowly I turned back toward the remaining three prisoners. There was terror in their faces as there must have been in my own. I know it was in my heart.

" 'Have you heard of this place called Cofitachequi?' I

asked, and I think that my voice quivered. 'The place with a woman chief? A land with plenty of the yellow metal?'

" 'Yes,' said one. 'I know of it.'

" 'Where is it then?' I asked.

" 'It's two days' walk from here. No more than that.'

" 'Which way?'

" 'North.'

"I turned back to face the governor again.

" 'The man told me that Cofitachequi is but two days north of here,' I said.

" 'Ah, that's more like it,' said De Soto. 'We'll set out immediately then to find this queen and all her gold.'

" 'Excellency,' said Gallegos, stepping quickly to the governor's side, 'the *caballos* will never make it. They need to rest and eat.'

"De Soto seemed to have a moment of quiet anger, but he overcame it. He turned his back on Gallegos, took a deep breath, exhaled with a heavy sigh, then faced him again.

" 'Yes, of course,' he said. 'How much time, do you think, the *caballos* will need?'

" 'Four days should do it, Excellency.'

" 'Then four days it is. We'll rest here in this place, this damned abandoned town, for four more days, and then we'll start out at the first sign of the Sun for Cofitachequi.

" 'Put these three in chains with the others. Search the town for food and anything else that we might need. Tell the men to select their houses for the time we'll be here.'

"My master García stepped almost immediately into a nearby doorway. He stood there and called me to him.

" 'This will be ours,' he said. 'Find Falda and bring her and my baggage here.'

" '*Sí, señor*,' I said, and I ran to find her. I had left the baggage with her when García had called me to serve as interpreter again. She was not far away, just back toward the edge of the village where we had come in. I found her there, lying on the ground beside the belongings of my master. She was very ill and too weak to stand or walk. Carefully I lifted her and carried her to where García waited.

" 'What is this?' he said.

" 'She's ill, master,' I said. 'She's very ill. May I put her inside?'

" 'No,' he said. 'Take another house. Take that one next door. No one has yet laid claim to it. Put her in there and get my things. Be quick about it.'

"I had somehow managed to fool myself up until that moment that my master was at least a little bit more human than the others. Perhaps that was because he had always protected me from them. But of course, he was only protecting his property. When I saw how unfeelingly he dismissed poor Falda, I knew that he was no better than Gallegos or even than De Soto, and I felt completely hopeless.

"I carried Falda into the house next to my master's and laid her on the cot in there as gently as I could. I knelt beside the cot and spoke to her in a low voice.

" 'Falda,' I said, 'can you hear me?'

" 'Yes,' she answered, but her voice was very weak and low. Her eyes were glazed, and I don't think that she could even see me.

" 'Falda,' I said, 'I have to leave you here, but I'll be back as soon as I can. Just rest. I'll be back.'

"I ran to get my master's belongings and put them in his house as quickly as I could. He was still standing there guarding the place. He stepped aside so I could get in with his things. I put down the bundle and turned to go out again.

" 'Where the hell do you think you are going?' he said.

" 'Falda,' I said. 'She—'

" 'Never mind about her. No one told you to go to her. Get my things unpacked. We're going to be here for four days.'

"I unpacked his things and put them around the house the way I knew he wanted them, but he kept finding things wrong and forcing me to make little unimportant corrections. He knew that I was worried about Falda, and I'm sure that he was keeping me from her on purpose. Why would he do that? I don't know. It was just another way of torturing an *Indio*, I think. I think that he enjoyed it.

"I kept wanting to say something to him, but I held my tongue. I knew that if I said anything, I would only anger him, and then I would never be allowed to go to her. So I tried to appear as if I was in no hurry, as if I were not really concerned.

"At last I was set free when Gallegos called out to my master from outside, and García went out to see what was wanted of him.

"I peeked cautiously out the door to watch, and the two men walked off shoulder to shoulder talking about something in low voices. I saw my opportunity and ran next door.

"When I got there, Falda was dead.

Eighteen

I DON'T KNOW why the death of Falda affected me so. I had seen more of death in the time I had spent with the Españols than I had ever thought I would see in my lifetime. And it had been brutal, violent death. I should have been used to it. I should have been hardened. But Falda's death saddened me very much. I had been frightened. I had been worried. I had been anxious. I had felt many things over the last months, years even, but following the death of Falda, I was sad and depressed. I no longer cared whether the Españols killed me or let me live.

"My master did not bother me much for those four days of rest. Nothing much was going on, and he had no need of my services. No one else dared bother me, for Capitán Viviano García was always nearby, and I was his property. If the Españols respect anything, it is personal property. I spent much time sitting in silence by myself, mourning the sad loss of Falda. She had been my companion in misery, and she had become, I realized too late, my friend.

"The four days passed without much incident, and early

on the morning of the fifth day, we started traveling again, still north, still searching for the place the Españols called the kingdom of gold. We had been on the trail again for two days when some of the Español soldiers came across three *Indios* and captured them. They brought them back to the main group and put them in chains with the others.

"In two more days we came to a wide and deep river, and we stopped there and made camp for the night. From the slaves the Españols had captured, they learned that just across the river was the territory of Cofitachequi. The crossing the next day was difficult, but I won't bother you with the details. It is enough for me to tell you that we crossed this one in canoes, and that when the men tried to swim their *sogwilis* across, seven of the animals were carried away and drowned.

"De Soto would not wait for all of his men and all of his *sikwas* to be taken across the river. He was much too anxious to see the 'Queen' and her yellow metal. He went across in the first canoe, taking Gallegos and García with him. I was taken across in the next one, for they needed me to use as interpreter.

"I think that there were only about twenty Españols and their *sogwilis* that headed for Talomeco, the central town of Cofitachequi. As anxious as the governor was, he did not want to appear that way, so they did not run the *sogwilis*, and I was able to keep up by trotting along beside them.

"When we went into Talomeco, the woman chief was there waiting for us. She was sitting in a litter chair which was held up by four men, and she was dressed beautifully in a mantle decorated with many different-colored feathers. De Soto rode up close to her chair and stopped his beast. The Queen, as the Españols insisted on calling her, was the first one to speak.

" 'So few?' she said, and I recognized her language. I don't think that it was *Chahta*, although it was very close to that language. I suppose that it could have been a dialect of *Chahta* with which I was not familiar. At any rate, I was able to understand, and when I responded in the language of the *Ani-Chahta*, she was able to understand me.

" 'These are only the leaders,' I said. 'Many more follow.'

" 'What are you saying there?' De Soto demanded. I told him what had transpired, and he was pleased at the way in which I had responded to the Queen. 'Tell her who I am,' he said, 'and tell her that I am the child of the Sun.'

"I did as he said, and the Queen smiled.

" 'Our neighbors, the Natchez People,' she said, 'claim that their ruler is the Sun himself. Is this man then the child of the Great Sun of the Natchez?'

"I could see that this woman was not impressed with De Soto's claim, and I myself suddenly had some doubts about the things that I had grown up believing, for as you know, we Real People say that the Sun is a female. It seems that everyone, every different people, has a different view of these things. Can we be right and all of the others wrong? I don't know. Perhaps no one is right about those great mysteries. I did know, though, that I did not want to translate her comment to the governor.

" 'She greets you and says that you are welcome here in Talomeco,' I told him.

" 'She does not appear to be frightened of me,' he said. 'She does not even seem to be impressed by our appearance and by our *caballos*.'

" 'My master wonders that you do not show more surprise at the appearance of these men,' I said to the Queen. I felt myself to be in a difficult situation, and I softened the words of both parties as I translated.

" 'We have seen their kind before,' she said. 'They're not new to us.' Then over her shoulder she spoke to a man who was standing in the street. 'Go and fetch the things that the other white men left behind them,' she said. The man turned and ran to do her bidding. While we waited for his return, I told the governor what she had said. The man returned with a few strands of shiny beads. Another man ran along beside him carrying two heavy metal axes. De Soto's eyes opened wide.

" 'Glass beads and iron axes,' said Gallegos.

" 'Ask how long they have had these things, talking slave,' said the governor, and so I did.

"The Queen looked around until she spied a child standing beside one of the houses. She made a gesture toward the child and spoke.

" 'Since about the time that one there was born,' she said.

"De Soto looked at Gallegos again. His brow was wrinkled as if in thought.

" 'How old is that boy, do you think, Gallegos?' he said.

" 'Oh, I would say, maybe twelve years,' Gallegos answered.

" 'Or thirteen maybe?' said De Soto.

" 'Yes. Thirteen. Of course. The lad must have been born in '26, the year of Ayllón's expedition. So Ayllón must have come through here.'

" 'Gallegos,' said the governor, 'we will go easy here—for a time. Make sure that all of the men get that word. I think that I may get farther with this Queen by smoothness than by other means. Tell everyone to mind their manners.'

" '*Sí*, Excellency.'

"Soon the rest of the troop, including the *sikwas*, arrived, and the governor gave orders for them to remain out of town. A large camp was established there, and only those of us who had arrived early stayed in the town. The Queen saw that we were given quarters, and a feast was served. Food was taken out to the camp for the others. Then we slept.

"We stayed several days in Talomeco, and the Españols committed none of their atrocities there. I thought that De Soto had been impressed by the power of the Queen, but I should have known better. One day I overheard a conversation between De Soto and Gallegos.

" 'I have been all over this town,' Gallegos was saying, 'and I have seen no sign of gold.'

" 'If Ayllón came through here, as it seems,' said De Soto, 'he would have taken all the gold for himself. Or if there were gold to be mined, he would have stayed. Would he not?'

" 'Yes,' said Gallegos, 'if he had found it.'

" 'If this Queen has gold,' said the governor, 'why does she not wear any? I don't believe that there is any gold here, or if there is, the bitch has hidden it all from us. Perhaps she hid it from Ayllón as well. She knew that we were coming, did she not?'

" 'Yes, of course she did,' said Gallegos. 'She had that huge feast prepared and waiting for us, and she herself was prepared to meet you.'

" 'Yes,' said the governor. 'Well, we'll wait a little longer. The rest will do the men and the animals good. Keep looking, but discreetly.'

"But the Españols found no gold, and after we had been there in Talomeco for twelve days, the governor's patience was at an end. He went to the Queen's house with several armed men. One of them was García. I was taken along to talk. The rest of the army was armed and waiting at the edge of the town. The friendly posture was at an end.

" 'Tell her to come out,' the governor said to me.

"I opened my mouth to call out to the woman, but apparently she had already heard us out there, and before I could shout, she stepped out through her doorway. She looked directly at me, and I ducked my head, both out of respect for her position and because of my own shame.

" 'What is this?' she said. 'Is this a way for guests to behave? Am I being threatened for some reason here in my own town?'

" 'This is the way these men usually behave,' I said to her, speaking the tongue of the *Chahtas*. 'I have been amazed that they waited this long to show you their normal behavior. They are very rude, brutal and bloodthirsty men. I am ashamed to be associated with them, but I am a captive and a slave. For your own sake, do not provoke them.'

" 'What do they want with me?'

" 'What are you talking about?' said De Soto, and his voice was stern and angry.

" 'She asks what you want here,' I said.

" 'Tell her that I am searching for gold. I came here because other people told me that hers was a golden province, but so far I've seen no gold here. Has she hidden her riches from me? Ask her that.'

" 'He's looking for the yellow metal,' I said. 'To these men the yellow metal is wealth. People to the south of us told him that he would find much of it here at Cofitachequi. Behind us in our path are many dead people and burned villages because this man failed to find the yellow metal he seeks. I fear for your town, your people and you, yourself, if he's not satisfied here in his search.'

" 'I see,' she said. 'Well, I have no yellow metal. Tell him that I will gladly show him all my riches if he wants to see them. The yellow metal is to be found north of here at Coco. We have none here.'

"I told the governor what the Queen had said, and I watched a frown harden his already ugly and scarred face, and the side of his face that wore the mark of Vitachuco began to twitch a little.

" 'Always farther north,' he said. 'Tell her to produce her wealth.'

"I told her, and she spoke over her shoulder. A woman came out of the house carrying a large basket with a lid. The Queen pointed to the ground in front of De Soto and told the woman to put the basket down and leave. She did. De Soto did not wait for an invitation. He stepped forward and jerked the lid off the basket, tossing it aside. The basket was filled with pearls. Gallegos gave a long whistle and stepped forward for a better look.

" 'Pearls,' he said. 'I've never seen so many pearls before.'

"De Soto shoved a hand deep into the basket and brought it up again. Pearls rained from his hand back down into the basket. A few remained in his palm, and he leaned forward to examine them very closely.

" 'Yes,' he said, 'pearls, but these pearls are the freshwater kind, not so valuable as the ones from the ocean, and not nearly so valuable as gold. We'll take them anyway. Ask the Queen where this Coco is and how far away.'

"I asked her, and she told me that it was the next territory to the north of hers. To get there we would have to travel through several of her villages and then cross another river. I passed this information on to De Soto.

" 'Good,' he said. 'We'll go there, and she will go with us to show the way and to escort us through her territory. Her subjects will give us no trouble if she's along. And of course, if she lies, and if I find no gold at Coco, she'll die at Coco. Tell her that, and tell her to get herself ready to travel at once.'

"So we started north again, this time with the Queen serving as our guide. She rode in her chair. When the four men carrying her could go no more, they were relieved by four others. Twenty men and as many women had been taken from Talomeco with the Queen. Her basket of pearls was on the chair with her.

"I tried to put the Queen and her possible fate out of my mind. After having suffered the loss of Falda, I did not think that I could bear to lose another person that I cared about. And the Queen was an admirable woman. She was not young, and I would not call her a beautiful woman. But she was handsome, and she had a dignity about her that was inspiring.

"I liked her almost at once, and I did not want to get to know her any better, for if I did, I was sure that I would like her better. That frightened me, for I could not imagine anything in her future other than an untimely death.

Nineteen

WE LEFT TALOMECO about the middle of the Españols' *Mayo*, the planting moon, and, as the governor had planned, we had no problems as long as we were within the territory of Cofitachequi. When we arrived at a village, the Queen gave the orders, and she was obeyed. De Soto was happy with the situation. Every town we came to, De Soto took more guides and bearers. Each town fed us as well as the animals. There was no resistance. No threats of force were required or used. The Queen got everything that De Soto wanted with just her word.

"The countryside was beginning to look very familiar to me, and I had a strong feeling that I was getting close to home, and so I became nervous and apprehensive. I did not think that I would be able to stand by as I had thus far, if the Españols attempted to slaughter my own people or to burn their homes.

"At the same time, I did not want to give myself away. I had never told the Españols, not even my master, Capitán Viviano García, where I had come from or to what people I belonged. I wondered if I would be able to keep that secret if we should go into a town of the Real People. Would someone recognize me and speak to me? I thought not, because I had been gone for so long and had aged so quickly. I was dressed in a strange manner, and my hair had grown long and was unkempt. Still, I was afraid.

"And I entertained thoughts of escape. I was so close to home. How could I allow myself to be taken away from it again? If the Españols even suspected that I was near my own home, they would watch me carefully, perhaps even put the collar and chain on me. I could not let them know.

"We crossed a river and then we were no longer in Cofitachequi. The Queen pointed out that fact to De Soto.

" 'I'm no longer of any use to you,' she said. 'We are beyond my lands. My people and I will go back now to Talomeco.'

"Of course, I had to translate that statement for the governor.

" 'I think not,' said De Soto. 'I still have use for the bearers, and as for you, you will make a fine prize for me to display back in Cuba, perhaps even back in España.'

"I turned to the Queen with my head low.

" 'He has no intention of releasing you,' I told her. 'He spoke of showing you off in his own land.'

" 'Then I am truly a captive?'

"It was as if a shadow passed over the face of the Queen, and I felt great pity for her and a terrible hatred for the governor.

" 'Be patient,' I said, almost without realizing what I was saying. 'I'll help you if I can.'

" 'But how can you? What can you do against so many?'

" 'I'll find a way,' I said. 'Be patient and trust me. I'll let you know when the time is right.'

"After I had said those things to her, I felt like a fool. I asked myself just how I thought I would manage what I had promised to do for her. Who did I think I was? Of course, she had been the cause of my sudden outburst of madness. When I looked at her and thought of her as a perpetual prisoner of these monsters from across the sea, I spoke without thinking. I believe, too, that Falda was there in my mind.

"I tried to stay away from her after that. I told myself that I did not want to take any chances on making the Españols suspicious by letting them see the two of us in conversation. Perhaps that was true. I think, though, that it was also true that I was trying to avoid her in case she asked me any questions about my plans. I had no plans. I felt foolish.

"We passed through two villages of *Ani-Chahta*, and then I knew that I was close to home. The governor took food from the people, but he took no more bearers or corn grinders. Perhaps he believed himself to be well enough provided for. In a few more days, I was sure that I was once again in the land of the Real People. I was thrilled, but of course, I could not show it, and I could say nothing to anyone about it. I was also worried about what might happen in my own land and about what I would do, if anything.

"We stopped at a village for the night, a village of the Real People, and I was called upon once again to act as interpreter. I had a moment of panic. I felt sure that my secret would be exposed. I stepped forward, and the town chief greeted me in my own language. It had been years since I had heard it spoken, and I almost responded before thinking. I tried to hide the joy I felt at hearing those beautiful sounds and at seeing my own people. And I did. I buried it in my fears. I could not speak the language without giving myself away.

" 'Do you speak the trade language?' I asked, speaking in that jargon.

" 'Yes, I do,' said the chief.

" 'These people would like some food and a place to sleep for the night,' I said, and I hoped that they would want nothing more. They fed us and gave us places to sleep, and in the morning, we left. I said a silent prayer of thanks.

"The next three nights we slept in camps out in the open country. We were turning west, moving away from the land of the Real People, and I was glad of that. While we were camped on the third night, I was walking back to my master's tent with water I had gotten from the river nearby. I had to pass close to the Queen, and as I did, I was stopped by an Español. His name was Ochone.

" 'Talking slave,' he said. 'What is it that García calls you? Juan José?'

" '*Sí, señor,*' I said. 'Juan José.'

" 'Juan José, will you help me for a moment?'

" 'Yes, if I can.'

" 'I want to speak to the Queen.'

" 'Oh,' I said, 'I don't know. Perhaps the governor would not approve of that. And I have to get this water back to my master.'

" 'Only a moment,' said Ochone. 'Please.'

"I had never before had an Español beg me or even speak politely to me. Perhaps that's what persuaded me to cooperate with him.

" 'What do you want to say?' I asked him.

" 'Tell her that I have never before seen such beauty as hers. Tell her that I would do anything for her. Tell her, please, that I am not like the others. I think that the governor is a pig for holding her captive. Tell her all those things for me, please. And tell her that I would spend the rest of my days in her service. Please tell her those things for me.'

"I told the Queen more or less what Ochone had said, and I noticed her raise an eyebrow. Nothing more.

" 'Then tell him to do something about it,' she said.

"I turned away from her and looked at the ground.

" 'Well?' said Ochone. 'Well, what did she say? Tell me, Juan José. Please.'

" 'She said that if you mean what you say, you should help her,' I said. 'You know, don't you, that the governor means to take her back to España with him? I have to go now. I'll be in trouble with my master.'

" 'Just a little longer,' said Ochone. 'A few words more.'

" 'I dare not,' I said. 'My master can be very impatient. I have to get back.'

"As I was walking away, I glanced back over my shoulder. Ochone was still standing there near the Queen. I imagine that he was trying desperately to find a way to communicate with her. I thought then that if I were to try to keep my own rash promise to her, perhaps this Ochone would be of some help. Perhaps after all it could be done.

"It was two days later, I think, that we had stopped on a plain to camp for the night. I was setting up my master's tent. García had left me alone. He had gone to the edge of the camp where the *sogwilis* were kept to take care of his own mount. Ochone approached me.

" 'Juan José,' he said, 'can I trust you?'

" 'Why, I don't know,' I stammered. 'Trust me with what? What do you mean?'

" 'I want to tell you something, but first I want your word that you won't repeat it to anyone.'

"I thought for a moment. It seemed a dangerous thing to do, to make such a promise. What if my master were to see me talking with this man and ask me what we had been discussing? If I gave Ochone my word, then I would have to lie to my master, and if I did that, would he know? I decided to take a chance on this Español.

" 'Tell me,' I said. 'I'll say nothing.'

" 'I'm going to desert.'

" 'Desert?' I said. I did not understand his meaning. I had not heard that word before.

" 'I'm going to run away in the night—secretly.'

"I made no reply. What should I say to such a confession? I kept at my work.

" 'I'm going to take the Queen with me,' Ochone added. 'And I want you to go with us. Will you?'

"I looked around frantically to see if anyone else might be near enough to hear what was being said. My head filled with images of terrible torture and death. I had been a slave for so long that the idea of making a decision on my own frightened me. The thought of my own freedom frightened me. I realized then that I had become a very timid old man. Then I thought of the Queen, and I thought of Falda.

" 'Yes,' I said, and I felt my heart begin to race from the fear that was inside of me. 'Yes, I will.'

"And so I was fully committed to the plan. I had already told the Queen that I would help her, and now I had agreed with Ochone to run away with him and the Queen. I wondered if we would make it, or if the three of us would die together at the hands of the scar-faced monster who led this mad expedition of death and destruction.

"It was two nights later when we again stopped on a plain to camp. It was still the planting moon. The soldiers were grumbling because we had found no villages to stop in. The night had turned cold. Some of the more important soldiers had small tents to sleep in, but most of them slept on the ground in the open when we were forced to camp out that way.

"We made our camp and lit small fires here and there, both for warmth and for light. Soon after dark, my master crawled into his small tent. I was left to sleep outside. Because of the cold, I lay near the fire. I was lost in a deep sleep when I felt someone shake me by the shoulder. My first thought was that it was early morning and my master was waking me to begin packing up his things for the new day's march.

"But it was not my master. It was Ochone. He whispered one word in my ear.

" 'Come,' he said.

"Trembling with fear and rubbing my eyes, I got myself to my feet. Ochone led the way, and I followed. He led me to where the Queen lay sleeping in her litter. Just there beside her was De Soto's tent. Ochone touched me lightly on the shoulder and pointed toward the Queen. I understood his meaning.

"I stepped quickly and quietly to her side, and did her as Ochone had done me, but as soon as I had touched her, she raised her head, and her eyes were wide open.

" 'Is it time?' she whispered.

" 'Yes,' I said.

"She got up, picked up her basket of pearls and followed Ochone. I walked behind her. There were guards around the camp, but Ochone knew where each was posted, and he managed to avoid them all. We crept through the camp to the far edge where the *sogwilis* were kept in a herd. A guard was there, too, but Ochone led us to the far side of the herd opposite the guard.

" 'Wait here,' he said, and crouching low, he moved toward the animals. I soon lost sight of him, for it was a dark night, and we were well away from the campfires. I felt very much alone and frightened, and I thought that Ochone was gone for a long time. I began to imagine that he had only invited us to run away with him so that we could be caught and punished. Then I saw him returning. He was leading two big *sogwilis*.

"When he got back to where he had left us, he just gave me a nod and kept moving. I and the Queen walked along beside him, away from the beasts. We walked in silence for a long while. At last Ochone stopped, when we could no longer see the red glow from the campfires along the far horizon behind us.

" 'I think we've walked far enough,' he said. 'No one will hear us now. Now we can ride.'

" 'We don't know how to ride your *caballos*,' I said.

" 'You don't need to know. I'll ride this one, and the Queen can ride with me. You can sit on the other, and I'll lead him. Just sit on his back. You don't have to worry about controlling him. We'll get much farther away much faster riding the *caballos*.'

"I was afraid, but I did not argue. Even though we had run away together, I was still inclined by habit to obey when told to do something by an Español soldier. I climbed on the back of the beast with some difficulty, and I admit that when it began to prance about I was terrified, but Ochone controlled it. In another moment he was mounted on the back of the other *sogwili*, and the Queen was sitting behind him. I don't know how they both got up there. I was too busy keeping my own seat to watch.

" 'Hold on, Juan José,' said Ochone, and suddenly the beast beneath me was moving. It seemed to me that we were racing blindly through the darkness, and I had fears that we might fall into a great chasm before we knew it was there. After a while Ochone slowed the beasts to a walk.

"We traveled all night that way. At daylight we stopped. We were on a rise overlooking a vast plain. There was no sign of any Español, except Ochone, of course, in any direction as far as we could see. We had made it. We had escaped. We were free.

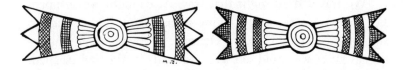

Twenty

AS WE MADE OUR WAY back to Cofitachequi, I kept thinking about De Soto and the others, wondering about their path of destruction. Where was it going? Who was in its way? How many more would be enslaved? How many die? The Españols were searching for a place called Coco. That was all I knew, and I did not know Coco. I did not know if it was a real place or simply a ruse that had been used to get the governor and his army to hurry on their way.

"We did not talk about De Soto, though. We talked of other things. How many days back to Cofitachequi? To Talomeco? One day as we rested from our travel, I noticed that Ochone seemed to be lost in thought. The Queen was standing a little ways ahead of us, staring toward her home. I sat down beside the *'squani*.

" 'Juan José,' he said, 'what will become of me, do you think, when we reach Talomeco? Will the *Indios* kill me there?'

" 'Why would they do that?' I said. 'You've saved the Queen.'

"He shrugged and sat in silence for a moment before he spoke again.

" 'Because of De Soto and Gallegos and the rest,' he said. 'Because of all the things they did. I was one of them.'

" 'No,' I said. 'I think you'll be all right at Talomeco. Unless the Españols come back.'

"As we traveled, I taught the trade language to Ochone, as much as I could, and he was not a bad student. Pretty soon he was talking to me only in that jargon, and he was at last talking directly to the Queen.

"But Ochone was not the only student, for the Queen and I each learned how to handle the big *caballos*, the *sogwilis*. All of this was good, for it made the journey seem to pass much more quickly.

"It was about the middle of the moon of green corn when we arrived back at Talomeco, and the people were overjoyed to see their Queen back alive and well. They welcomed Ochone and me as her saviors, and we were both informed that we had a home there with them at Talomeco for as long as we might want it.

"I was overwhelmed by my own sense of liberty. I had been a slave for so long that I just enjoyed doing nothing and sitting alone and thinking about the fact that I was being idle on purpose and that there was no one to chastise me for it. The grateful people of Talomeco took good care of me, and they expected nothing of me in return. They treated me like a respected elder. I stayed around there resting and getting fat until the moon of corn in tassel was about halfway through.

"By then my brain was tired of being idle. It was thinking a great deal about De Soto and his victims. I had escaped along with the Queen and Ochone, but what of all the others? What of the victims yet to come? I began to feel guilty about my own good fortune. I was also curious about the activities of the *Ani-Asquani*. I decided that I could remain idle in Talomeco no longer.

"When I announced to Ochone and the Queen that I intended to leave, I neglected to tell them my real plans. I said that I had a need to return to my own people. Ochone gave me one of the *sogwilis* to ride, and the townspeople outfitted me well for a long trip. I rode north, searching for the trail of De Soto.

"At first I only retraced our own steps back to the campsite from which we had escaped. De Soto, of course, was long gone from there by the time I made it back. But his trail was easy to find. I had only to follow the droppings of the *sikwas*.

"I passed through a town called Guasili, where the people told me that they had given the *'squanis* three hundred dogs for food. I crossed a large river the way I had seen some of the soldiers do, by holding on to the *sogwili* as it swam. I was afraid at first, but it turned out to be a very easy thing to do.

"I came to a place called Chiaha and discovered that the Españols had spent over twenty days there, and the governor had been up to his old tricks. People there were still in mourning. Some were dead and others had been carried away in collars and chains. Their supplies, too, were considerably diminished.

"It occurred to me that if I was not careful, because of De Soto's occasional long stops for rest, I might catch up with the governor and his army before I realized it. I decided I would have to be more cautious from this point on, for I was traveling much faster than were they. I was one mounted man, traveling alone, unburdened.

"The people of Chiaha, in spite of their recent losses, resupplied me for the trail. I spent the night with them and left again the following morning. The droppings along the trail were fresher than before. I was catching up with the *sikwa* herd. De Soto and the mounted soldiers were probably a little farther ahead. I should see them before much longer. Determined, I rode on.

"Early in the moon of the end of fruit I came to a place called Acoste. The chief there was named Coste, and his town was on an island in the middle of a river. A resident of the town took me across in his canoe. While I was there, Coste told me the story of De Soto's visit to his town.

" 'I had heard of this man's exploits and of his cruelty,' said Coste, 'and I knew that he was coming this way. So I prepared for him. I had many warriors ready to meet the white men: some from this town, some from other towns nearby. They were all well armed, and they were placed all over the town and even in places outside of town. Some of them were out where they could be seen. Others were concealed.

" 'When the white men came near, I myself went out to meet them. I invited them into my town, and if they had acted the way guests should have done, there would have been no trouble. It was my intention to greet these men as a friend, but I did not mean to suffer at their hands the way I had heard others have suffered. I was prepared to act as host or enemy. The choice was theirs.

" 'The leader of these men, De Soto, an ugly man with a scar on the side of his face, and some of his men came into town with me, and they started to steal from us right away, grabbing food and other things that caught their eye. One of them rudely took hold of one of my young women. I shouted to my warriors, and they showed themselves.

" 'Then De Soto changed his face. He began to beat his own men and shout at them. He did this, I think, to keep me from telling my warriors to attack. He was greatly outnumbered. The biggest part of his army was still across the water from us.

" 'I made them make their camp across the water from us, and I told De Soto, through one of his slaves who could speak the trade language, that there is a land north of here called Chisca where he might find the yellow metal he searches for. He sent two of his men to find it, but they came back in two days and said that the way was too rough for their big riding animals to travel.

" 'After spending seven days in his camp across the water from us, he left. You can tell where they camped by the mess that is still there.'

" 'Yes,' I said. 'I saw the mess they left.'

"In the nut moon I reached a place called Tasqui where I was fed and given shelter for the night. The *Ani-Asquani* had passed through there as well. Then I traveled for several days without seeing another village, but I was still on the trail of De Soto. It was still clearly marked by the droppings of the *sikwas.*

"It was the harvest moon and getting cold again when I found the place called Coco. It was a real place after all, and De Soto and all his people and animals had been there before me. They had stayed four days. I found it difficult to understand why the place was not a heap of ashes, for De Soto had been told that he'd find the yellow metal at that place. He had not, of course. I asked the people there about it, but they didn't seem to understand my question.

" 'He asked for food,' they said. 'We fed them and they left.'

"They fed me, too, and then I left. For several days after

that I was never in unsettled country. The towns were numerous and close together, and in between were cultivated fields. I stopped at one place where they told me that the governor had taken many people away in collars and chains.

"Shortly after that I came to a swollen river, and near the river I found ample evidence that the Españols had camped there several days. I imagine that they had been waiting for the river to go down, but it did not. I tried to figure out how they had crossed. They had not built a bridge. There were no large trees nearby to cut. I saw no raft along the bank on the other side. They must have gotten canoes from one of the nearby villages and taken them across.

"I studied the river, wondering how I would get myself to the other side. Should I hold the *sogwili* and let him swim? This river was much wider than the one I had crossed before in that manner, and the waters were more swift. If I were to lose my grip and be separated from the animal, I would almost surely drown. I have never been a good swimmer. I decided that I must have a canoe.

"I rode alongside the river to the nearest village and bartered for one, a heavy dugout similar to the ones we make. I left the *sogwili*. As I walked back toward the river dragging the canoe, I heard a hideous noise behind me. I turned to look and saw that they were shooting the beast full of arrows.

"I went on, got my canoe into the water and crossed to the other side. As I pulled my canoe up out of the water, I was startled by a loud squeal from behind me. I turned, and there I saw a *sikwa* running loose. I wondered how many of those strange animals were wandering around now on their own.

"At the first town I found on the other side of the river, I discovered that De Soto and his men had carried away thirty women. In eight more days I found another place. The same thing had happened there. About that same time, I saw another *sikwa* running loose.

"The next two nights I spent in the open, sleeping on the ground. Then I came upon an old abandoned town. It was fenced, and there was evidence that the Españols had stopped in there to rest. I was glad that it had been abandoned long ago. I was also glad to have its shelter, for the nights were getting cold. I moved into a house for the night and built myself a fire. My food supply was getting low. Before I left the town I saw that several *sikwas* had moved in.

"For the next few days I visited a number of different towns where De Soto and his army had passed through. His behavior, it seemed to me, had become peculiar and totally unpredictable. At some towns he did not even bother to stop. At others he spent the night or even several days. In some towns he did not molest the people, while he took prisoners from others.

"I was fed in all these places, and my supplies for the trail were replaced. All of the people I encountered were friendly to me. Perhaps they had had enough of rudeness from the Españols.

"Then one night I slept alone beside a river, and as I lay there slowly drifting off to sleep, I asked myself why I was following this trail. Why had I not gone home, as I had told my friends back at Talomeco I would do? I was consumed with curiosity about De Soto. That much I knew. But did I want to see the damage that he did? I had seen enough of that. Did I want to know the end result of his expedition? What would I do if and when I caught up with my prey?

"I did not know. I did decide that I had to see the end of the story. I had been there at the beginning, and I felt like I had to know the rest. I finally went to sleep, and in the morning I found a log and used it to hold me up as I swam across the river.

"On the other side I found a *sogwili* running loose. I tried to catch it, but it ran each time I got close. I wasted half a day in this manner. I had learned to ride, but I still don't know how the Españols manage to catch those beasts.

"In the middle of the next day I came to the top of a rise, and then I saw the *sikwa* herd. De Soto could not be too far ahead.

Twenty-one

I T TOOK ME two whole days to work my way around
the *sikwas* and all the herdsmen with them, and then I
discovered that there was a great distance between them and
the lead group of soldiers. I hurried ahead, but I watched
carefully as I moved, for I knew well that there were often
lone scouts or groups of four out scouting around away from
the main body.

"I did not see De Soto and the men with him until the end
of that second day when the darkness had come. Then I saw
the glow of their campfires along the horizon ahead of me.
At this point I had to be very careful. De Soto and his
mounted soldiers were ahead of me, foot soldiers and swineherds behind.

"I followed them in this manner for two more days, and I
saw them enter another occupied village. From my distance,
I was unable to tell anything about their behavior there.
They stayed there for three days, though. The next day's
march failed to take them to another town, and they camped

that night in a forest. I kept my distance and watched carefully. I was getting very tired.

"The following day after about a half a day's march, some *Indios*, as they say, came to meet them. They met in front of a village that was walled around, but it was not the village of the people who had come to meet De Soto. They conversed there in front of the walled town for a while, and then they left, the *Indios* leading the way.

"It seemed obvious to me that yet another town chief, hearing of De Soto's approach, had sent messengers to invite them to his town and to guide them there. I followed them at a safe distance, always watching behind me as well.

"It was another day's journey to the town, which I later found out was called Mabila. It was a large town, probably the mother town of a whole region, and the region was heavily populated. Several towns were nearby. There was a wooded knoll not too far from the town, and there I hid myself away to watch.

"De Soto and his men moved in. I couldn't tell for sure, but it looked to me as if they were securing houses for their own use. The people there made a feast that night, and there was dancing and singing as well.

"The Españols did stay for a few days, and then the others arrived, so that they were all together again. The swine, or *sikwas*, were kept outside of the town where a few men were required to stay with them to watch them or chase them when they strayed. The other men all moved into the town, taking with them most of their slaves, bearers and corn grinders. It looked as if the *'squanis* meant to stay for a while.

"My own food supply was dwindling once again, and I began to worry that I would have to leave my secret place to look for food before the journey was resumed. But then one morning I saw a struggle in the town. I couldn't tell exactly what had happened, but it was plain enough to see that *'squani* soldiers were scuffling with *Indios* down there. Then there were shouts. Then things seemed to quiet down again.

"But as I watched, I could see that something was afoot. Many armed *Indios* appeared in the town, and the *'squanis* began to stealthily withdraw. Before the end of the day, there were clearly two armed camps facing each other and preparing to do battle. Warriors from other towns nearby came into Mabila as well.

"I cannot truthfully say who it was, which side, that actually began the battle. All at once, it seemed to me, I heard the loud bangs of the *'squani* guns, and I saw a sky full of arrows come at the *'squanis* from the group of *Indios* gathered there before the town.

"It matters little, though, who actually began this particular fight. The important thing is that the Españols were guests at best, invaders intent to conquer at worst. The *Indios* were in their own homes.

"I have given this matter much thought, and it seems to me that all of the people the *'squanis* call *Indios* would have been much better off had they killed all of the white men who showed up in this land on the first big boat. That is a violation of our code of behavior toward strangers, I know. But this time, I think, it would have been for the best.

"Of course, it does not matter what might have been. The events of the past are done. The present is what it is. And then too, perhaps it was all supposed to happen just as it did. I'm not wise enough to know these things.

"Whatever the case, the battle was on. For a while they kept their distance from each other and fired back and forth. The Españols fired their guns a few times, but those things are almost useless. The big noise frightens people when they first hear it, but after that the guns are no good.

"So both sides were shooting arrows at each other. Many arrows struck their marks. From my hiding place, I could see *'squanis* and *Indios* hit by arrows. Some were only hurt. Others dropped when hit, obviously killed.

"Then the riding soldiers on their mounts screamed a hideous war cry and raced toward the defenders of the city. As the big beasts came toward them, the *Indios* scattered. Some shot arrows at the riders from a distance, and I saw at least two riders fall from the backs of their *sogwilis* with arrows sticking in their bodies. Some of the animals, too, were struck by arrows, and their screams were horrible to hear.

"When the mounted soldiers reached the edge of the town and their targets had already scattered in all directions, they pulled back on the reins of their mounts to slow them down or halt them. They turned, looking for someone to chase and attack. While they were thus confused and the beasts were stamping around, some of the *Indios* who had run away came back to attack.

"They swung warclubs at the mounted Españols or tried to drag them from the backs of their *sogwilis*. Some were successful. The Españols, too, had deadly war axes with which they hacked at their opponents. Some ran at them with their long lances. It was the most ferocious battle I had yet seen, and many were hurt or dead on both sides. Never had the invaders suffered so much at the hands of their victims.

"De Soto himself was knocked down, badly hurt, and would surely have been killed had not two of his men caught hold of him and dragged him back to safety. I saw my former master shot through the shoulder by an arrow. Staggering, he managed to save himself. Gallegos was bloody all over, but I could not tell from where I watched if the blood was his own or someone else's.

"As more people were killed and hurt on both sides, the battle began to slow. *Indios* and *'squanis* alike withdrew. If you asked me who it was that won the fight, I couldn't say. I could only say that there were more dead *Indios* than dead Españols. But there were eighteen white men slain. I counted the bodies from where I hid. I could also see the same number of dead *sogwilis*. And the *sikwas?* There were many killed.

"I waited until after dark, and then I crept in close, going through the village and keeping in the darkest shadows. The Españols were in their camp outside. The *Indios* had run away. I got as close as I could to the Españols and still feel somewhat safe, and I could hear some voices. I don't know who was speaking, but there were two at least in conversation.

" 'The governor is furious,' said the one. 'Four hundred of his precious pigs are dead.'

" 'Well,' said the other. 'We should have bacon in the morning. Or sausage at least.'

" 'I doubt it,' said the first. 'More likely it will be a mass burial with a prayer said over all the remains.'

" 'We lost eighteen horses and eighteen men,' said the other. 'How many hurt? Have you heard?'

" 'Every man of us is hurt. I heard the captain say that the hundred and fifty of us left have had seven hundred wounds. I have three myself.'

" 'You got off easy. I have five.'

" 'Some are pretty badly hurt. More will die yet from this bloody fight. You'll see.'

" 'How badly hurt is the governor?'

" 'Pretty bad, I guess, but then not bad enough, I say. I think he'll live, unless his wound should fester.'

" 'How many savages do they say we killed?'

" 'Two thousand five hundred is the figure that the governor will report. That's what I heard.'

" 'There weren't that many altogether, if you ask me.'

" 'So he'll report a lie. It won't be the first, I imagine.'

" 'Well, we're going back, I heard.'

" 'Yes, and with nothing to show for it but scars and missing limbs. Have you heard when we'll be leaving?'

" 'We'll lie around and lick our wounds awhile, I guess, and then we'll head back south toward the sea. Our ships are waiting there for us, so the governor says. We'll see.'

"They stayed there for twenty-six days. I counted each and every one. A few more men died there while they waited. The *Indios* did not return, but every now and then I noticed that they were watching to see what these Españols would do. At last—it was the middle of the big trading moon—they started in to march again. Many of them limped or hobbled. They all moved more slowly than before. Only about one hundred *sikwas* followed. I followed too, at a safe distance behind.

"They traveled not south, but southwest, and some of the country they led me through began to look familiar to me. It made me think of the land I had traveled through many years earlier with my two companion priests just before we were captured by the Fierce People. We were not yet that far west, but we were going in that direction. The thought of the Fierce People made me feel uneasy, but I continued to follow the *Ani-Asquani*.

"They traveled into and through the moon of snow, and it did, indeed, snow. It snowed very hard for several days, and travel was stopped. The Españols made themselves a camp, and the winter cold was hard on them. A few died. I found where someone had dropped his burden along the trail, and I took it.

"Inside the bundle I found some clothes. As much as I hated dressing myself again like a '*squani* slave, the clothes were warmer than what I was wearing. I also found some food and a knife. And there were some blankets. With these things I was able to make myself a little camp and to keep reasonably warm. I was still some distance behind De Soto and his men.

"When the snow began to melt, they started to travel again. They still moved slowly because of their wounds and the sickness that had been brought on by some of the wounds. And the *sikwas* slowed them down as well. De Soto was no longer leaving the *sikwas* and the swineherds and the foot soldiers to keep up as best they could. His numbers were too much diminished, so he kept them all together.

"They moved on throughout the moon of cold and into the moon of bony. Then they came across an abandoned town, and they moved into it to rest for a while. I camped nearby and kept my watch on them.

"In the windy moon they started out again, but they were going west. I think that they were lost, for after traveling several days, they turned and headed southeast. In another few days, they headed southwest again.

"I managed to get closer to them during the moon of flowers. They seemed to be wandering almost aimlessly. They no longer watched carefully or scouted the way soldiers do. They argued much among themselves. I got the idea that the men wanted to kill some *sikwas*, but De Soto wouldn't allow it. They traveled on.

"At last they arrived at a village, and there the people gave them food. The Españols were so weak that they did not threaten the people there. They accepted the food and moved on. But once again, they headed west. They seemed to argue even more among themselves.

"It was in the planting moon when De Soto and his men reached the edge of the big river. I remembered it from my first trip west. It was very wide and it was high and running fast. They stopped there and set up a camp. The *sikwas* started running wild, and no one tried to stop them. I watched from hiding still, and one day I saw some men put something long and heavy into the water. It was all wrapped up, so I could not really see it, but I thought that it looked like the body of a man.

"I wondered why they had put it in the river. I had not seen them do that before with their dead. I thought perhaps I was wrong, and that it had been something else altogether. I stayed hidden and watched, and then I saw that the Españols began to slaughter the *sikwas.* Every man, it seemed, was trying to kill at least one of the squealing beasts.

"They butchered them and cooked the flesh over open fires, and for three days they did nothing but kill *sikwas* and cook and eat them. Some of the animals escaped, of course, to run wild into the countryside.

"Then they left. They headed south along the bank of the big river. I watched them go, and I was going to follow them still farther, but first I went to the camp they had abandoned. They had left much behind. I was looking through the things that they had left to see if there was anything that I could use, when I heard a groan come from inside a tiny tent.

"I thought of running away. Then I went to the tent and peeked inside. There was Capitán Viviano García, my former master, lying on his back. There was dried blood all over the front of his chest, and there was mixed in with it dried, caked, yellow pus. His face was sickly yellow, and his lips were swollen, dried and cracked. His breath was raspy.

" *'Capitán,'* I said, 'can you hear me?'

" 'Juan José? Juan José, is that you?'

" 'Yes,' I said, 'it is.'

" 'Where have you been, you bastard?' he said.

" 'Never mind,' I said. 'It looks to me like you've been left to die.'

" 'Yes. To die.'

" 'Your governor,' I said, 'is a fine one to leave you like this. That's the kind of man you follow.'

" 'Not the governor,' he said.

" 'What?'

" 'De Soto's dead. We dumped his body in the river.'

Twenty-two

I STAYED THERE with García for four more days until he died, and then I did with him what he and the others had done with their governor. I wrapped him in the blankets from his tent and dumped his body in the big river. I did not follow the others, for De Soto was dead, and they were going home. They had killed hundreds of *Indios*, tortured hundreds more and burned dozens of towns. They had left people without homes and without food. They had left children without parents, wives without husbands and husbands without wives. I think that the land they traveled through will never be the same again.

"I decided then that it was time for me to return to my home, but I was alone, and I knew that I was a long ways off. I kept on the clothes of an Español slave, for by this time I had no others. In the abandoned camp I found a broken lance, and that I picked up to use as a staff. I thought about picking up other things to bring back and show, but I decided against that. I wanted to travel light.

"I walked for two days, and then I came across a *sogwili*

that was loose. It did not run from me when I approached it. I mounted it with some difficulty and rode. I rode for several days. I don't know how many, but after a while I traded the animal to a man in a village beside a river. I traded for a canoe, and after that I traveled by water. It was much faster except when the rivers did not take me in the right direction. Then I walked.

"I was close to home when I finally abandoned my canoe and walked the rest of the way. When I was nearing Men's Town, or the place where Men's Town used to be, I knew that I could go no farther. Then I found that Men's Town, like so many other towns that I had seen in recent days, was gone—burned to the ground. I did not know what had happened to it. I lay down there in the ashes expecting to die there where I had once lived so many years ago.

"You know what happened next. My story's done. De Soto's dead. The men who followed him are gone. But I believe that more will come. I wanted to tell you my story to warn you of what can happen when these strangers come into our land. Be prepared. My story's done."

Deadwood Lighter sat down slowly and carefully, his weary old bones creaking as they bent. He appeared to be exhausted from his tale. Dancing Rabbit got up from his seat and went to his old companion's side. The townhouse at Kituwah was more crowded with people than it had ever been before, yet it was silent. The people all were stunned.

'Squani sat staring at the ground between his feet, lost in his own special confusion. He was filled with fascination for the people of his unknown father. At the same time, he was horrified at the deeds described by Deadwood Lighter. He, himself, felt perfectly human. As human as anyone else. How could his own father, then, have been inhuman? It just did not make sense.

"My friend," said Deadwood Lighter, his voice now weak, "I'm tired. I need to rest."

"Come on," said Dancing Rabbit. "I'll take you to my sister's house. You can rest there and eat. Come on."

Deadwood Lighter allowed Dancing Rabbit to help him back up to his feet and to escort him out of the townhouse. The people inside sat still. Only those crowded around the doorway moved to allow the two former priests to leave the building. Then from the back of the room, a voice spoke quietly.

"It was my town he visited with those people. I saw them. Of course, at the time, we did not know that Deadwood Lighter was with them."

"Everything he has spoken is true," said another. "I've heard stories from the *Ani-Chahta* and the *Ani-Tsiksa.*"

"I met a man who had been traveling," said another. "He had seen one of the towns that the *'squanis* burned."

Just then, 'Squani got up and left the townhouse. No one paid much attention to his exit. They had begun to talk among themselves in small groups. At last one man got up and walked to the front. He held out his arms asking for quiet and attention.

"What will we do about the white men," he said, "if, as the old *Kutani* says, more of them come?"

"We'll fight them," called out someone from the back of the crowd.

"You heard about the fights with these men," said another.

Another man stepped up and moved to the front.

"We'll close the mountain passes," he said. "We'll close them all around. I and my clansmen, the Wolf People. No one will come into the country of the Real People. The Wolf Clan will close it to the outside world, if all of you agree."

And so terrible had been the tale of Deadwood Lighter,

and so fresh in the minds of the Real People were the ghastly images of what the De Soto expedition had done, that the voice of the People was unanimous. The proposal of the Wolf Clan was accepted. The land of the Real People would be closed off to the rest of the world.

Glossary

Cherokee words and phrases used in *The Long Way Home*

Ama-edohi   *ama*, water + *edohi*, he is going, "water walker" or "sailor."

Ani-Asquani   Spaniards (*ani*, plural prefix + *Asquani*, a Spaniard). The Cherokee word is possibly a result of Cherokee attempts to pronounce the Spanish *Español*.

Ani-Chahta   Choctaw People, or Choctaws.

Ani-Cusa   Creek (or Muskogee) People, or Creeks.

Ani-guhnage   black people (*ani* + *guhnage*, black).

Ani-Kutani   the *Kutani*, an ancient priesthood of the Cherokees. The word *Kutani* cannot be translated.

Anisguhti   the planting moon, May.

Ani-Tsiksa   Chickasaws, or Chickasaw People.

Ani-yunwi-ya   the Real People, the Cherokee designation for themselves (*ani*, plural prefix + *yunwi*, people + *ya*, real or original).

Anuhyi   windy moon, March.

Asquani   a Spaniard. See *Ani-Asquani*.

Dulisdi   nut, the moon of nut, September.

Duninuhdi   the harvest moon, October.

Galoni   the moon of the end of fruit, August.

Gatayusti   an ancient Cherokee gambling game, played with a disc-shaped stone and a spear.

Gihli   dog.

Gola   the cold part of the year.

Guhnage   black.

Guye quoni   the moon of corn in tassel, July.

Jisdu   rabbit.

Kakali   the bony moon, February.

Kawoni   the flower moon, April.

Kutani   a priest. See *Ani-Kutani*.

Nuhdadewi   the big trading moon, November.

Sikwa   this word originally meant an opossum, but when the Spaniards introduced the pig, the Cherokees applied the word to the pig and began calling the possum a grinning possum *(sikwa utsetsasdi)*.

Sogwili   horse. Literally, he is carrying it on his back.

'Squani   a contraction for the word *Asquani*, Spaniard.

Tihaluyi   the moon of the green corn, June.

Uhsgiyi   the snow moon, December.

Unoluhdani   the cold moon, January.

Wado   thank you.

Yansa   buffalo.

ABOUT THE AUTHOR

Robert J. Conley is a writer who specializes in Cherokee lore. He is the author of several previous novels, including *The Way of the Priests*, *The Dark Way*, *The White Path*, and *The Way South*. He has received Spur Awards from the Western Writers of America for his 1987 short story "Yellow Bird," and for his 1992 novel *Nickajack*. He lives in Tahlequah, Oklahoma.

ABOUT THE ILLUSTRATOR

Painter/pipemaker Murv Jacob, a descendant of the Kentucky Cherokees, lives and works in Tahlequah, Oklahoma. His meticulously researched, brightly colored, intricate work centers on the traditional Southeastern cultures and has won numerous awards.